Dennis Koranek

The New Adventures of
Starr Gazer

A Christian Fantasy Novel

Print ISBN: 978-1-66783-462-7
eBook ISBN: 978-1-66783-463-4

To the glory of God

Table of Contents

Acknowledgments

I'd like to thank those that have made this second book possible.

- My son Simeon who had spent time reading the text to provide initial comments early on.
- My sister Diane who encouraged me to finally get this published.
- Betty Gray Thompson who volunteered to provide the needed proofing and editing close to publishing time.

Preface

God works in mysterious ways. The first paragraph of the Preface of my previous book, *"From Lightning to the Light"* was as follows:

"There are no such things as coincidences in life. God is in control of everything. He takes care of the sparrows and knows how many hairs are on our heads. Things that happen in our lives that we question may have happened the way they did because God has planned events to carry out a specific purpose. We wonder why people are sick or die at times that may be premature. Sometimes we find out the answer and sometimes we don't. The Lord may bring people into our lives at certain times for a single purpose and then we are left wondering why. We may or may not ever find out."

That paragraph continues to be very true, and in the age we live in, if we didn't have God to rely on, our lives would appear to be meaningless, and we would go through life in despair with no hope for the future.

In this book, we see that Starr continues to have adventures where it is apparent that God has put her in those situations for a reason. Some situations relate to war and minimizing the loss of life, others bring people closer to God by making it blatantly obvious that God is real, and still others allow the love of Christ to be shown through humbleness and mercy.

Enjoy,

Dennis R. Koranek

Part I

The First Xtreme Christmas

Chapter 1

The Think Tank

Evelyn had been busily working on the report that her boss was expecting when she heard the beeping sound from her computer's electronic calendar. As she looked up to clear the reminder, she shook her head.

"Looks like I'll have to remind the boss about the board meeting in a few minutes."

Evelyn quickly saved the electronic file for the report since she never knew when there would be a power glitch. Her boss was one that thought highly enough of the engineers to get them an Uninterruptible Power Supply (UPS) since an interruption in their work could cause a large drop in productivity, but he was a real Scrooge when it came to the administrative support staff. She got up from her desk and walked to the large closed door that was only about 10 feet from her desk. She knocked on the door and then immediately opened it and entered.

"Excuse me, Mr. Crawford, but the meeting with the board is in 10 minutes in the Manassas room."

"Thank you, Evelyn," replied the CEO. "I'll be right there."

"Sir, you know they don't like to be kept waiting."

A smile from the boss was all it took for Evelyn to get the message. She left the office and thought to herself, "He can't blame me if he's late."

Brad Crawford was the billionaire CEO of Crawford Enterprises, a high tech think tank devoted to technology that "pushed the envelope" that was considered to be "well beyond state of the art". He was not only a highly respected businessman but was also a technological wizard. That combination is very hard to beat. Brad had been interested in technology from an early age and always won blue ribbons at science fairs. His fame started when he came up with the idea for an oven that could thoroughly cook any kind of food in less than a minute without burning it. He started a small company, hired an advertising firm and outsourced the manufacturing portion. Housewives were immediately drawn to this invention, and Brad sold millions of units making him an instant millionaire. Business grew at an exponential rate for some time since he continuously came up with new inventions.

Though Brad was a very demanding boss, the company employees were loyal to him. They knew that he had great ideas for products and that if they stuck with him, their future would be secure.

The meeting with the board today was to be quite routine. Brad would tell them that the stock was continuing to rise at better than 50% per year and that he saw no end in sight. This would please them to no end and the meeting should be over within an hour.

Brad got up from his executive chair, walked over to the office door, opened it and proceeded to walk by Evelyn's desk.

"Sir, you have 2 minutes."

With a sigh, Brad responded with, "Thank you, Miss Markham."

"One more thing, sir. You've received an invitation to be the guest speaker at the UVA convocation next week."

"Kind of short notice isn't it? They probably had somebody back out at the last minute."

"I think you're right sir."

"Tell them I'll bail them out. It'll be a great way to talk to the kids about their possible future with Crawford Enterprises."

Evelyn just shook her head and sarcastically replied, "Whatever you say, sir."

As Brad walked down the hall he responded in a loud voice, "That's the attitude Miss Markham."

Twenty six seconds later Brad opened the door to the Manassas conference room and immediately went to the head of the table. There were six other people in the room, five sitting at the table and one working at a computer at the far end. There were three gentlemen in business suits, two women in business suits and one woman in her early 40's at the computer.

"Good morning, everyone," said Brad in a loud and commanding voice. "Let's get to business. The company has made a 50% profit every month this year, and with the new super high efficiency house plans and appliances we are about to roll out, our profits are only expected to climb even higher."

One particular business woman spoke up. "I've seen the plans and prototypes for these units, and I'm very impressed. As a mother and keeper of a house myself, I can't wait to try them out. They should reduce energy consumption, all are very eye appealing and they should cut down on the workload of the buyers rather dramatically."

This was all that the rest of the board members needed to hear. One man started to clap his hands, and then the rest of the board followed.

With that, Brad smiled and said, "Unless anyone else has something to bring up, I suggest we adjourn the meeting."

All agreed and the meeting was adjourned.

On the way back to his office, Brad was intercepted by Evelyn. "Excuse me sir, but the local food bank has asked us to make a donation to help the needy at Thanksgiving. What should I tell them?"

Brad shook his head as he walked past her and was about to enter his office. "Tell them we don't believe in the basic principle of Thanksgiving and all the religious stuff that accompanies it." Brad finished entering his office and closed the door.

Evelyn just shook her head and in a loud voice, but not expecting to be heard, declared, "Whatever you say, sir."

A couple of thoughts came to Brad's mind. "That's another board meeting I can check off," he said with a rather pleased look on his face. A few seconds later he began thinking about the group wanting money for Thanksgiving. He shook his head from side to side and said, "When will these people learn that there is no God and that all the time, money, and fighting these people do in the name of religion is a total waste of time? If these wretched people would have gone to school like they should have and had a good education, they could have been a benefit to society instead of a burden. They might have even been lucky enough to get a job with Crawford Enterprises." This made him smirk and then laugh quite loud.

Evelyn heard the laughter coming from the boss's office and just shook her head. Brad in the meantime started thinking about what sort of speech to give to the students. He wanted to promote

Crawford Enterprises but didn't want to come across like such a task master that none of them would want to work for him.

"Okay, let's see what I can come up with. I should talk about how the future is in their hands, and the decisions they make will decide the kind of life and retirement they will have, that working hard really does pay, how slacking off will not get them very far, and they should continue their education so they won't get stagnant in their field. Even getting additional Bachelor's degrees to broaden their knowledge is better than just wasting their life away."

This seemed to please him to no end, and he was quite satisfied with his preparation, however small. He was always very confident, and this came out in his speeches.

Evelyn knocked on the door and then walked right in.

"Sir, another social service agency called. Even though Christmas is a little ways away, they want to know if we would like to make any donations to support children whose fathers are in jail."

Brad just looked at Evelyn with his head cocked and quite stern. Evelyn decided to be proactive this time.

"Should I just take care of it and give them a similar story as the last group?"

This made Brad smile, shake his head in the affirmative and respond with, "Evelyn, I'll make a manager out of you yet."

Evelyn left the room to respond to the agency, and Brad just smiled saying to himself, "For someone without a major education, she has some promise. I'll need to review her salary and likely give her a raise. Maybe I'll suggest that she go back to school and get an MBA."

Chapter 2

Financial Problems

Pastor Bob Tanner had been the part time pastor of Greene Community Church for 10 years. When he arrived, there were about 50 regular attendees, and now there were only about 25. It was nothing in particular that he did wrong, the drop in attendance was seen among all the churches in not only this county but also the surrounding ones. The likely contributing factors included people moving to the city instead of the country, people wanting more pizazz in their services, and just the basic fact that people have so much going on (sports, work, and entertainment) that they no longer had time for God. It wasn't like the people were being asked to spend Sunday morning, night, Wednesday night and other nights of the week at church, they were just being asked to come Sunday morning for Sunday school and church. Since some sports events were now taking place on Sunday for children, people simply decided that was more important than attending church. The lack of people attending church seemed to make the attending congregation depressed and wonder why they should even keep the church open.

It was Monday night, and Bob was getting ready for the leadership board meeting. During dinner, Bob looked at his wife Sue with a very concerned look. She didn't normally see him in this state and decided to reach out for his hand. Seeing her hand extended, he smiled, and then reached out for her hand.

"What's the matter honey?" she said. "This isn't like you."

With a big sigh, he replied, "I'm concerned about the church, it's in financial trouble and I think we may have to close if we don't get some ideas on how to bring in some money. I already don't take a salary and the piano player doesn't take any money. We had to take out a loan just to make basic repairs to the building and we're having trouble paying that off. The $400/month that's required for the next few years is really killing us when you only take in about $800/month. The church has nothing in savings and the checking account is now costing us $5/month just to keep it open. It's not as if we can bail the church out since we're living on the edge ourselves."

Sue smiled, gripped her husband's hand tight and said, "Has the Lord ever let us down before?"

Sue was a very loving wife and made an excellent pastor's wife. She was in her mid 30's, had shoulder length chestnut brown hair and generally preferred long skirts and dresses to pants. This served multiple purposes. It was something she really liked, was more comfortable, and also happened to keep the congregation from gossiping. Though she had a Bachelor's degree in social work, she had decided to stay home and care for the children until they were out of college. She had seen too many problems with children whose parents both worked full time outside the home since many of the parents left the house early, didn't get back till evening, and were continually gone on business trips.

After a few seconds, Bob responded with a smile and a "Never once, dear."

With that, Bob looked at his watch and said, "It's about time for that meeting."

Bob got up, kissed his wife goodbye and walked to the door. Their four children were pretty young in age - 2, 4, 5, and 9. Amazingly, they had all been exceptionally quiet during dinner, and it wasn't till their father walked to the door that they started speaking up. The 5 year old girl spoke up first saying, "Dad, what about our kisses?"

Their father smiled, walked over to each of them and gave them a kiss on the top of the head after which he left the house.

***

The leadership board was already at the church in the Fellowship Hall when Bob arrived. Out of the five people that were already in the room, the only one that smiled and said hello was a man in his 50s with hair that was just starting to gray.

"Hello, Pastor Bob. This is the day the Lord has given us. Isn't it wonderful?"

Bob had a hard time to argue with someone as continually positive as Johnny Taylor. Johnny always had a smile, and Bob had never seen him with a negative outlook. Johnny was a part time farmer and a full time mechanic. The saying around the county was, "If it's broke, get Johnny, he can fix it." Though his children were now grown and out of the house, Johnny still didn't have any money since he always gave it to people in need. His favorite statement was, "Don't worry about me, the Lord will provide."

"Yes, Johnny, this is a good day," Bob replied as he tried to force a smile. Bob went to sit at the table and begin the meeting. The others included Jennifer as the board chair, James as the treasurer, Margaret as the clerk, Ken as the head of the deacons and Johnny as the head of outreach. Since many in the church had left, there was only one other deacon in the church.

"Okay everyone," declared Jennifer. "Let's call this meeting to order so we can get home in less than 2 hours. James, what's our current financial state?"

"Our loan balance is $17,483.47. Our current checking account balance is $645.34. The water heater just sprung a leak and Johnny says he can't fix it since it rusted through. It will cost about $350 to put in a new one."

"Can we put that off?" asked Jennifer.

"Maybe," replied Ken. "But I wouldn't put it off too much if we want to have any fund raiser dinners here."

"That's a pretty good point," responded Jennifer as she shook her head in the affirmative.

"So that leaves us with a little under $300," James continued. "If we want to continue the one outreach we have of providing some weekly groceries to the neighborhood needy, we won't have a whole lot left."

"Regardless of what else we do, we can't stop outreach. That's the one thing we can personally do to help the county and spread the Gospel, and it's the one thing the Lord has called us to do," Johnny reminded the group.

They all knew that he was right and nodded their heads.

"Okay everyone, so what do you recommend?" asked Jennifer.

"I'd say the first thing we do is ask the Lord for direction," said Johnny. "You realize that we didn't even start this meeting off with prayer."

"Of course you're right," acknowledged Bob.

The rest of the group agreed and asked Johnny to lead the group in prayer.

"Lord, we know that there are no coincidences in life and that you are always in control. We know that if You want this church to survive that You will find a way to make that happen. Please guide us to make all the right decisions and do not let us stray from the direction You would have us go. Please give us peace of mind so we may rest in the fact that whatever the outcome, we know that it will be the decision that You want and not just what we want. In Jesus' name we pray this. Amen."

As the group opened their eyes, they felt a little better and decided to adjourn the meeting and wait to see over the next couple of weeks whether any of them had any inspiration from the Lord.

As Bob drove home, he felt shaky and decided to pull over. He felt as if the Holy Spirit was talking to him and then as if by magic, he had an idea for a sermon. It wasn't his normal sermon in any sense. This was to be a sermon like no other he had ever given. He couldn't wait to get back home to tell Sue. What he didn't understand was that since everyone in the church was saved and though this sermon should be great, he wasn't sure why he needed to give it at this point in time.

When Bob arrived home, he tucked the children in bed and then took Sue by the hand and walked over to the couch and sat down with her.

"Honey, the church is even lower on money than we thought. Johnny prayed and all of us felt much better about the outlook though we didn't know why. On the way home, the Holy Spirit gave me some ideas for a sermon and though I don't know why, I'm going to need to spend a lot of time preparing for it."

"I felt like there was something special that was going to happen. I was praying for all of you while you were at the meeting," responded Sue.

Bob smiled and then leaned over and kissed Sue. "I knew I married the right person."

After a few seconds, Sue asked Bob the obvious question, "So, what is the amazing sermon going to be about?"

"The basic topic will be 'Why don't people believe, and even once they do, why aren't they doing anything?'"

"Wow! That should be a good one," exclaimed Sue. "I'm glad I'll be there."

"Just pray for me this week and whoever it is that needs to hear this sermon."

Chapter 3

Rescued

Brad decided to spend a little time at work prior to going to the convocation. The convocation wasn't till 2PM and though it would take him a couple of hours to get there, he still figured that he had till about 11AM before he had to leave. Since it was only 9AM now, he could get a couple of hours of work in, and at the same time he could check on who was actually in plant this particular Saturday. As he was walking around some of the engineering cubicles, he saw one particular engineer in her early 20's, and seeing the name Natalie on the cubicle wall decided to strike up a conversation.

"Good morning, Natalie," said Brad in a professional, yet friendly voice.

With an extreme look of surprise, the girl looked at Brad and opened her eyes wide.

Seeing that he must have startled the poor girl, Brad spoke back up. "I'm sorry, did I surprise you?"

Once Natalie got over her shock, she replied. "Yes sir. I just don't normally see too many people here on Saturday."

"Do you work most Saturdays?"

"Since I'm not married and don't have a family, I thought I'd work and learn as much as I can while I have the time."

"Good philosophy, Miss Stewart. Keep up the good work."

"Thank you sir, I will."

Brad left Natalie to work and walked a little more before returning to his office. He started thinking about Natalie as he walked and thought to himself, "Nice girl, Natalie. Good work ethic. I'll have to check on her salary and engineering grade level."

When Brad got back to his office he brought up Natalie's records on his computer which had a wireless interface. Brad spoke to himself as though there was another person in the room. "Says here she just graduated last May, and this was her first job out of college. A few modifications here, a few there and presto. She just got a promotion, raise, and an achievement award. I bet she'll be surprised when she gets her next paycheck."

Brad always liked to reward employees that he thought were particularly industrious and loyal. That's some of what the employees liked about him.

After another hour, he decided it was time to head off to the convocation. As he drove along, he thought about some new inventions and decided to record his thoughts using his in-car computer microphone that provided pretty good speech-to-text even with considerable background noise. He had found this program on-line and found that the author was a 16 year old boy named Jim Skyler from Kentucky. Brad offered the boy a summer intern position a few years earlier and the boy worked for him every summer since. Brad really liked him and decided to offer him a full 4 year scholarship to any college in the country. Jim liked Brad as well and took him up on the offer.

On a normal day Brad would have parked in the parking garage but on this particular day being the guest speaker, he was allowed to park much closer to the event. As he got out of his car, he was met by one of the students specifically assigned to meet his needs.

"Good afternoon, Mr. Crawford," declared a young man in a professional business suit. "I'm Michael Gibson and I've been assigned to get you safely to your destination and meet any particular need you have before commencement."

"Thank you, Michael. I don't have too many needs. Point me in the right direction, show me where the bathroom is, make sure I have some water available and I should be just fine."

"Right this way, sir."

As they began walking toward the building where the commencement was to be Brad decided to find out a little bit about Michael.

"So, Michael, tell me a little about yourself."

"I'm a junior here at UVA majoring in Mechanical Engineering with a minor in Physics and specializing in holography."

"Well, that sounds like a promising career. How's your GPA?"

"It's currently at 3.76, and I'm hoping to bring it up next year. I've signed up for graduate courses during my senior year, and I'm hoping I haven't bitten off more than I can chew."

"I'm sure you'll do just fine," replied Brad. "Do you have a job for the summer yet?"

"I had one with G Labs, but when they started laying people off due to a contract loss, they had to rescind the offer."

"You seem like a smart lad, how'd you like an intern position with Crawford Enterprises this summer?"

Michael stopped in his tracks and didn't speak for a few seconds since he was totally in shock.

"Do you really mean it?"

"I never say anything I don't mean."

"Yes, I would love the chance to work at Crawford Enterprises for the summer."

"When can you start?"

"Would a week from Monday be okay? I'll need to finish up here and coordinate getting a place to live."

"That'll be fine. Call my secretary, Evelyn Markham, on Monday, and she'll arrange everything for your arrival the following Monday."

"Thank you sir. My volunteering for this assignment turned out even better than I thought."

"Truthfully, anyone that volunteered to follow me around for the day deserves something for the effort."

That started Michael laughing, and even Brad chuckled a little.

By this time they had arrived at their destination, and Michael directed Brad to where his seat on the stage would be. Michael whispered to Brad that the person at the podium arranging his notes was the president of the university, Dr. Tom Mitchum. Michael and Brad walked over to the podium, and Michael proceeded to work on the introductions.

Looking at Dr. Mitchum and pointing to Brad, Michael said, "Dr. Mitchum, this is Mr. Crawford." Then pointing to Brad, Michael said, "Mr. Crawford, this is Dr. Mitchum."

"Very nice to meet you, Mr. Crawford. The ceremony is just about to start and as you can see, the students are just filing in.

Once they're seated, I'll begin the ceremony, and once the graduates receive their diplomas, I would appreciate it if you would say a few words."

"How long will I have?"

"If there's any way you can keep it to 15 minutes, I'm sure all the students and their families would appreciate it."

"Shouldn't be too much of a problem."

The basic ceremony was uneventful, but the whole group seemed a little uncomfortable since this was an outdoor ceremony, and the temperature was close to 100 degrees Fahrenheit.

As Dr. Mitchum finished his speech, he began Brad's introduction.

"Most of you know of the man I'm about to introduce. He has revolutionized the way we prepare our meals and is known for being a man of integrity with good business sense. He began with virtually nothing and in a few short years, he's one of the richest and most powerful men in the world. I introduce, Mr. Brad Crawford, CEO of Crawford Enterprises."

The entire assembly stood and applauded. Brad went to the podium, shook the hand of Dr. Mitchum and began to address the crowd.

"Thank you Dr. Mitchum, and the entire assembly for the opportunity to speak to you today. Oh, by the way, the last time I checked, I was the richest man in the world," Brad said chuckling.

Brad then turned back to the audience. "Believe it or not, as college graduates, you are now considered adults by the majority of the world population. In short, this means you have a responsibility to act like an adult. In other words...act your age, and you will gain the respect of the people you meet."

"Just because you've graduated, it doesn't mean you should stop learning either. I recommend going further with your education, whether it be a Master's or Doctorate, a second Bachelor's or even technical certificates. The world is waiting for your contribution to society."

"What does it mean to contribute to society? Yes, you can make money by inventing something that people want or by providing a service that is for something frivolous, but if you want to make lots of money and feel a true sense of satisfaction, you need to make something or provide a service that the world really needs...in other words, something that it can't do without. This may or may not be anything that you'll do right out of school, but it is important that you continually look for these opportunities. The moment that you stop dreaming about ways to improve society, that will be your downfall, and you'll likely amount to nothing and may even be close to an early grave."

"Keeping fit is another thing that will help you in the long run. A sharp mind is developed and enhanced by what you eat and how well your cardiovascular system is maintained. A calorie of sugar and a calorie of protein isn't used by the body the same way. Your body needs a variety of good food to help you work, and a couch potato that eats popcorn and empty calories will not be productive. Though I do believe in productive employees, I also believe they need sleep occasionally. Unless there's an emergency, employees need at least half their day away from work."

"Even if your body is deteriorating with age, it doesn't mean that you have to check out of society. You can still eat well, and you can pass on to others the wealth of your experience. People will make the same mistakes if not sternly told the likely results. Yes, most people will still make mistakes and not likely listen to the voice of experience, but it is still important to warn people of potential outcomes."

"Since I'm not one for long speeches, I'll close with this. You are the future of the world. Just as the lives of us older folks will soon be in your hands, there will come a day that some of you may be up here speaking to a group of college graduates, and your lives will eventually be in their hands. If you're responsible and develop a respect for others, others will develop a respect for you. One last thing, maintain your integrity. Say what you'll do, and do what you say. Follow through on your promises, and you will gain the respect of many. Thank you...and by the way... remember to apply to Crawford Enterprises. We're always looking for new talent."

Brad stepped away from the podium, and the entire audience stood and applauded at which point Dr. Mitchum and other distinguished members of the University took turns shaking Brad's hand. Michael was last and escorted Brad off the stage.

"Thank you for taking the time to speak to us, Mr. Crawford," said Michael. "I'm sure that everyone was quite happy to listen to your thoughts."

"Truthfully, I expect that the graduates were most likely grateful for the short speech. Very little that a commencement speaker says really penetrates beyond the outer ears."

Michael didn't quite know what to say, but after a few seconds he couldn't help himself and started to chuckle.

"It's quite alright Michael, though I meant what I said in both my last comment and at the commencement, laughing is quite appropriate at the moment."

Soon they arrived at Brad's car, and the two parted with a last comment from Brad. "See you a week from Monday. I always take the time to meet the new employees."

"Yes sir," Michael said with a smile. "Thank you and have a safe trip back home."

Brad smiled and started the journey home.

Johnny was always in a good mood and thoroughly enjoyed spending time with his wife, Linda. Now that their children were grown, both of them were able to spend more time together and tried to do as much together as time would allow including night time Bible reading and prayer. She got a part time job with the local Social Services agency once their children were grown so that she could bring in a little extra money and still be at home when Johnny was. The love that they had for each other and for God was obvious to anyone that knew them.

"Honey, I need to go get some parts for the church furnace down in Charlottesville. I'd love to have some company. You up for a little drive? There may even be an ice cream cone in it for you."

Linda gave her husband a very loving smile and replied, "I would be honored to be accompanied by such a handsome gentleman on a lovely day like today."

They both laughed and gave each other a hug as they got ready to leave.

Traffic was relatively light as Brad made his way back up Route 29. Brad always had a lot on his mind and was in the process of coming up with a new invention to clean floors. While traveling through a densely wooded area of Greene County, several does and fawns darted across the road. Brad did not have time to react other than swerving and though he avoided collisions with other cars, he went into the grassy median strip over a small hill, across the opposing lanes of traffic and into the ditch on the opposite side of the road facing the opposite direction. Dirt was flying everywhere and when the car came to a stop, Brad was extremely shaken and found he couldn't open any of the doors or windows. He had also made the car windows bullet proof making it even more difficult to try and get out of the car. Due to where the car was located, nobody could see it from the road. Brad tried everything he could think of including honking the horn (which didn't work). What was worse was that there was smoke coming from the front of the car and Brad was hoping that a fire wouldn't start. On a last ditch effort Brad decided to try flashing his lights in a continuous SOS pattern to try to get the attention of someone. The car was pointed away from the road thus the lights were not going to do much good.

Johnny had always been an observant type and ever the resourceful one. As he and Linda started down route 29 from Ruckersville, something happened to catch his eye. On the left he noticed lots of grass and dirt that looked pretty fresh, and on the right he noticed dirt, torn up grass and car tracks that seemed to go over the embankment. As he slowed down Linda asked, "What's the matter honey? Why are you stopping?"

"It's probably nothing. It just seems a little weird all this dirt and torn up grass. Looks pretty fresh. I'll check it out and be back in a jiffy," replied Johnny as he got out of the car.

As Johnny looked over into the ditch which was at least 15 feet down, he saw Brad's car. He motioned to Linda to get out of the car while he went down the bank into the ditch to Brad's car to see what the situation was. After Linda got out of the car, Johnny was already most of the way to Brad's mangled car.

"Honey, I'm going to check this out. Please throw me any tools that I need."

"Okay dear," came the reply.

Johnny got to Brad's now smoking car and knocked on the window to get Brad's attention. "Can you hear me?" Johnny asked.

"Yes," replied Brad. "The doors and windows are stuck and the windows are bullet proof."

Johnny thought for a second and called up to Linda, "Honey, can you throw me my special glass cutter? The one that's in the tool box in the top left compartment."

About 30 seconds later, Linda put her hand up with the tool in it and asked, "Is this the one?"

"That's the ticket, Lassie," he replied. "Can you throw it down?"

She always had a good aim and managed to toss it within a foot of him.

"Thanks, honey."

Johnny picked up the tool and immediately went to work on the driver's side window. This tool he made was specifically used for cutting and fitting bullet proof glass. As a mechanic, he sometimes needed to help deal with problems for special police cars or other dignitaries.

As Johnny completed the last portion of the cut, he shouted to Brad, "Turn your head away from the window. I'm going to hit it with the tool and it should fall onto you in one piece."

Brad shook his head in the affirmative and turned away.

With one quick blow, Johnny hit the window, and it fell inside the car in one piece just touching Brad's shoulder.

Brad turned to Johnny and while attempting to get his seatbelt off, he realized that it was stuck.

"The seatbelt locking mechanism is stuck," Brad nervously shouted to Johnny.

In a split second, Johnny pulled his Emergency Medical Technician (EMT) pocket knife from his pocket and flipped up the seatbelt cutter. In just a few more seconds he grabbed the seatbelt and ripped the shoulder belt first followed by the lap belt.

"Okay, you should be able to just slide yourself through the window," said Johnny.

Brad nodded his head and started pulling himself out of the car with Johnny's help. After Brad was half way out the window, a spark from some of the frayed electrical wires hit the paper sitting on the passenger seat and ignited it. By the time Brad was all the way out, most of the passenger seat was on fire.

"I smell gasoline," shouted Johnny. "I think it's going to blow soon."

Brad nodded and the two men ran toward Johnny's car as quick as they could. Before they got half way, the car exploded and the blast knocked them to the ground. By the time that they picked themselves up off the ground, a police car had arrived and a crowd had gathered.

After the policeman got out of the car, he came down the embankment and approached the two men. As he was about to speak, a fire truck arrived and the firemen started getting out of the truck.

The policeman was the first to speak.

"Hello, Johnny. Which of you can tell me what happened?"

Brad spoke up first. "The car is mine, officer. Some deer darted across the road on the north bound lane, and when I swerved to avoid them, the car hit some dirt in the median, and I ended up crossing the south bound lane and finally ended up in the ditch here. The car doors, windows, and seatbelt jammed, and I was trapped. If it wasn't for this man, I'd have been dead."

Brad looked at Johnny and said, "By the way, I never did get your full name."

"Johnny Taylor, and my wife up there on the hill is Linda," replied Johnny.

"Well, I owe you a big one for the rescue."

The officer asked Brad some questions, and once the fire was out, and the firemen left, the policeman spoke up one last time.

"Mr. Crawford, do you need a ride somewhere?"

Before Brad could get a word out, Johnny spoke up.

"It's okay, officer, I can get him wherever he needs to go."

The officer smiled at Johnny and said, "Mr. Crawford, you're in good hands with Johnny here."

With that, the officer winked at Johnny and left.

Johnny looked at Brad and said, "Okay, Mr. Crawford. Where do you want to go?"

"Are there any car rental places in the area?"

"Yes, just a few miles down the road near Airport Road."

"That'll be fine."

The two men got back to Johnny's car, Brad sat in the back seat, Johnny and Linda in the front seats, and they headed for the car rental agency.

A few minutes later, Brad spoke up and said, "Thank you for saving my life."

"All in a day's work," replied Johnny. "The Lord was good to us both."

Brad looked at Johnny from the back seat, shook his head with a sarcastic look but said nothing.

A few minutes later they approached the car rental agency and Brad spoke up again.

"I'd like to give you something for all your trouble. Would you take a check for $1000?"

"Shoot, Mr. Crawford, I really don't want any money."

"Everybody wants something. Name your price."

Johnny thought for a minute and replied, "I'd be honored if you came to church with us tomorrow."

Brad quickly replied, "I'm an atheist. I really don't believe in all that religious stuff. I believe we all evolved from lower life forms. Religion is for superstitious people that don't have enough education to know better."

Brad quickly realized that he put his foot in his mouth and attempted to back pedal a little. "What I meant was that people are entitled to their opinion. If people want to believe in religion they can, if they don't want to, they don't have to."

Though Johnny was slightly taken back, he knew how to witness to people and remained calm.

Brad decided to keep on talking. "So what can I really do for you? I won't take nothing for an answer."

Johnny smiled and responded, "My request still stands. Honey, get some paper out, and give the man the directions to the church along with the time for Sunday School and the service."

Linda pulled out some paper and began writing down the information. When she finished, she gave Brad the sheet.

Though Brad had no intention of going to the service, he knew better than to put his foot in his mouth a second time.

Johnny pulled into the rental agency parking lot, and though Brad got out, the others stayed in the vehicle. Before Brad closed the back door, he spoke up one last time. "Thank you again for the rescue."

With a smile on his face Johnny replied, "See you at church tomorrow, Mr. Crawford."

Brad just smiled and shut the door. After completing the paperwork for the car rental he drove toward his home in Northern Virginia. He spoke to himself as he drove, "I think I could use a good rest...I think I'll sleep in tomorrow."

After Linda and Johnny finished shopping, a puzzled Linda spoke to her husband.

"Honey, do you think we'll see Mr. Crawford at church tomorrow?"

"I've been praying about it, and I honestly believe he'll be there."

"I certainly hope you're right. He could use Jesus in his life."

"Amen to that."

Chapter 4

The Service

It was 2AM on Sunday morning, and Brad had been sleeping restlessly. He kept having recurring nightmares where he relived the car accident from the previous day. It always ended with Johnny's request, "I'd be honored if you came to church with us tomorrow." followed by Brad's response.

Each time that Brad woke up from the nightmare he'd say, "It's only a dream. Though Johnny did a good deed, he'll eventually get over my not being at church with him today."

By the time that 6AM rolled around, Brad was exhausted. He decided to get up, make breakfast and watch the news. There was nothing particularly exciting happening in the news, so he decided to catch up on some paperwork. As he turned on his computer and the desktop flashed, for a split second he saw Johnny on the screen.

"This is just too weird," he said shaking his head from side to side. "I've got to get this out of my mind."

By this time it was getting close to 8AM and Brad said to himself, "Well, I couldn't make Sunday School even if I left right now."

Then out of the blue he started feeling guilty. His subconscious started talking to him, and he realized that he continuously talked about integrity and how important it was to stick to your word. Then he curved his mouth in a smirk and said, "How bad can this be? I'll have a nice little drive, sit there for an hour and leave. I'll have kept my commitment and I'll be home by 2PM. I'll even be able to sleep tonight. Let's see, it's 8:26. By the time I get ready it'll be close to 9:00. It'll take about 2 hours to get there so I should be just about in time for the service."

He thought for a minute and said to himself, "And if I don't hurry up, I won't make that."

After a minute he said, "At least I read up enough on religious practices to realize the difference between Sunday School and a service."

Linda and Johnny were getting ready for church and Linda spoke up saying, "Honey, I've been thinking about that man we helped yesterday. Do you think that he'll show up today?"

"I feel in my bones that he'll show up."

Linda looked at him with some apprehension but gave her husband a loving hug.

Sunday School started with six adults and the only children being Bob and Sue's. Linda looked at her husband and catching her glance, he knew what she was thinking.

"Lots of people don't go to Sunday School," said Johnny, "especially when they're coming to a new church."

Sarcastically, Linda replied, "But he's never been to church. He doesn't know the difference between Sunday School and a morning service."

"Have faith young woman, have faith."

Linda smiled and just shook her head.

Brad arrived at the church at 10:50 and sat in the car for a few minutes trying to decide what to do. So there wouldn't be any real hullabaloo when he went in, he decided to wait till 10:58 to go in the building. When he walked in, he realized that there were only about 20 people in attendance. He saw Johnny and his wife, a woman with 4 children, a woman in her early twenties, a man at the pulpit, and the rest well over 60 years old. Brad thought he'd sit in the back and hope that few people noticed him. When Johnny heard the door close, he turned around, saw Brad and immediately stood up and began walking over to him.

"Welcome to our church, Mr. Crawford," greeted Johnny as he extended his hand for a greeting.

Brad nodded and shook Johnny's hand.

"You're welcome to come sit with my wife and me."

As soon as he blurted that out, Bob's 5 year old daughter saw Brad, jumped out of her seat and came running toward them. The little girl knew that if Johnny was talking to the man that it must be okay for her to be friendly as well. Her parents had always told her never to be scared since Jesus was always with her, and He wanted her to talk to people about Him.

"Hi, my name is Faith."

Faith held out her hand and grabbed Brad's.

"It's okay. You can sit with me. I'll tell you what to do and show you the ropes. My daddy is the pastor."

Brad didn't quite know what to say. He looked at Johnny who was ready to burst out laughing at this point and who managed to just smile and say, "It's okay. We can talk after the service."

Faith led Brad over to the pew where her mother and siblings were. There were 3 columns of seats. One on each side and one in the middle with about 10 rows in each column. As they entered the pew which was in the third row middle section, Sue looked up and though surprised, welcomed the stranger into her pew. As soon as he was settled, Bob started the service with Faith still clinging onto Brad.

"Good morning, everyone. Isn't it a beautiful day that the Lord has made? Let us rejoice and be glad. Let us start by singing Hymn number 152, *We Gather Together*. Since our regular pianist, Mrs. Juniper, is still in the hospital, we'll need to sing acapella unless there is someone else that is willing to play."

Brad could read music very well, and though he wasn't exactly a professional, could sing reasonably well and play a couple of instruments including the piano, viola, and a little trombone. After hearing the request for a piano player he decided to lay low. He didn't want any more attention drawn to himself then there already was.

Faith opened the hymnal and found number 152. She held it up for Brad to see, and though she was only five years old and had only been reading a short while, she tried her best to sing along with everyone else.

When Brad saw how Faith was really trying to help him, he smiled and began singing along. It was obvious he could carry a tune and with his voice projecting so well, everyone began to sing their best.

When the Hymn was over, Bob welcomed everyone including the visitor.

When the welcome was complete, Bob said "Are there any joys or concerns?"

Johnny raised his hand and Bob acknowledged him to speak.

"I'd like to praise the Lord that Mr. Crawford came out of the accident in one piece yesterday and that he blessed us all by coming to church today."

The whole church began clapping which embarrassed Brad all the more.

Once the clapping stopped, Bob continued saying, "Anyone else...joys or concerns?"

Sue spoke up with, "Mrs. Juniper isn't doing very well. She has pneumonia, and after her treatments for cancer, her white blood cell count is very low."

"We'll keep her in our thoughts and prayers."

"Anyone else?" asked Bob.

Linda spoke up. "We need to keep the church itself in our prayers. We're awfully low on money."

When there was nobody else, Bob said, "The scripture reading today is taken from Proverbs chapter 3.

My son, forget not my law; but let thine heart keep my commandments:

For length of days, and long life, and peace, shall they add to thee.

Let not mercy and truth forsake thee; bind them about thy neck; write them upon the table of thine heart:

So shalt thou find favour and good understanding in the sight of God and man.

Trust in the Lord with all thine heart; and lean not unto thine own understanding.

In all thy ways acknowledge him, and he shall direct thy paths.

Be not wise in thine own eyes; fear the Lord, and depart from evil.

It shall be health to thy navel, and marrow to thy bones.

Honour the Lord with thy substance, and with the firstfruits of all thine increase;

So shall thy barns be filled with plenty, and thy presses shall burst out with new wine.

My son, despise not the chastening of the Lord; neither be weary of his correction;

For whom the Lord loveth he correcteth; even as a father the son in whom he delighteth.

Happy is the man that findeth wisdom, and the man that getteth understanding."

Bob paused for a moment and said, "This is the word of the Lord. May the Lord bless the people who hear and heed His word."

With that, the ushers came forward and took up the collection. Brad, realizing that it would look bad if he didn't put anything in the collection plate, put a token $10 in it.

Once the collection was over, Bob said, "Let us stand and sing Hymn 253, *All Hail the Power of Jesus' Name.*"

Faith smiled at Brad and found the new hymn. Brad was touched by the child's mannerisms and decided to reach out his hand to her this time. She took his hand and then gave him a hug which totally took him by surprise.

When the hymn was finished, Bob began his sermon.

"Why don't people believe that there is a God and if they do believe, why aren't they acting like it?"

Brad looked like he'd seen a ghost. How did this man know that he was an atheist? Did Johnny tell him? He couldn't have come up with a sermon that quickly.

Faith saw that Brad looked a little nervous and decided that she needed to comfort him by leaning up against him and holding his arm. Brad looked at Faith and smiled. Her touch almost seemed to make him feel a little better.

Bob continued.

"How many people here like to be in control of their lives? Go ahead don't feel shy, you can raise your hand."

A few people raised their hands, and although Brad knew his answer, he kept his hands down.

After people lowered their hands, Bob continued again.

"Though I might step on a few toes, why do you think so many women have trouble in the birth process? Let's go back to Exodus chapter 1 verse 17. We see that the midwives feared God. Though the explanation they gave to Pharaoh was that the mothers were so physically fit that they gave birth easily, that was not the whole answer. Is it just that the women were in good shape? No! These women had a real faith in God. They allowed God to be in control instead of themselves. Fear has a way of creating stress and when people have a lot of stress, it takes a toll on their body. In normal situations people can handle it, but in childbirth, the body needs relaxation and not stress.

"Many women today have trouble with the birth process because they refuse to let God be in control and let their bodies do what He meant it to do at the proper time. This is how God intended it. How impatient we are! The times we live in are very much an 'I always want to be in control' time. People like to have control over their destiny and the outcome of any situation. Women in labor do not like to feel they are out of control. So...what happens? Everyone gets impatient, fear takes over, the monitors see fetal distress, and cesareans occur far too frequently. Or for that matter, some people simply opt for cesareans from the start so that they can be in control at all times.

"This 'control' is a direct result of the 'me' generation. I am the most important thing in the world, and nothing else matters. This is the direct opposite of what Christianity teaches, and it is the same with people's attitude toward God. People want to feel they are in control of their lives. If there is a God, then they would need to be accountable to someone for their actions. People don't like that. It is different in a job because people feel they can quit if they really want to...whenever they feel like it and only subject themselves to control as long as they feel a need to do so.

"It goes like this. If people have to believe in a God, then they would be responsible for their actions to someone who sees what they do all the time. There would be no hiding what they do. If they choose not to believe, then these people reason that they are no longer accountable for their actions and can do as they please within the confines of the law.

"Since the beginning of time people never wanted to be accountable for their actions. What these people do not understand is that the truth does not change based on your belief. If I adamantly told you that 5+5=8.2 because that was what the average of all the answers I got from polling first graders, you'd say that I was crazy. You know that 5+5=10.

"If I told you that George Washington never lived because I never saw him, you'd say that he did because the history books say so.

"The Bible says that Jesus lived on the earth, and it talked about creation but people don't believe it because science tends to say otherwise. I tell you that science needs to learn how to interpret what the Bible says about creation.

"Let's take a few concrete examples. Evolutionists believe in theories like the Big Bang, or the expanding/contracting universe. The problem with an expanding/contracting universe is that something had to kick off the reaction. The laws of motion indicate that items at rest tend to stay at rest unless acted on by an outside force. Something had to put an energy mass out in space for a Big Bang to take place. Turn in your Bibles to Psalm 104 verse 2. *Who coverest thyself with light as with a garment: who stretchest out the heavens like a curtain.* Just think about this for a moment. In essence, this describes how God stretched the heavens when he created them. If science knew how to interpret this they would realize that objects that are stretched (e.g. rubber bands) keep themselves over the distance they are stretched. The same is true with light. When light is stretched like it describes in this passage, you get a redi-made universe that seems like it is older than it really appears using today's scientific methods. Another analogy would be that God likes baseball and decided to throw (pitch) the stars to their locations. As the stars went to their new locations the light stayed along the path. Those people that like the expanding theory might like the fact that the stars haven't stopped moving.

"What's the definition of science? One of the definitions of science indicates that something can be proven again and again by repeated experimentation. It's hard to do that with the universe, but scientists believe that through looking at things like stars they feel they are looking at the far past, and the past is so far back that it had to be millions of years ago. They also believe that carbon dating is essentially linear. What would happen if it weren't? What would happen if God created a universe that appeared to have age embedded into it?

"It all comes down to faith. I believe that there's a God because I couldn't fathom any other logical way for everything to be created. If I think about the consequences of unbelief (that is, Hell), I simply wouldn't want to take the chance of being wrong. Forever is an awful long time to gamble on something this important.

"Belief is such a simple thing. It is not just saying that God exists. Even Satan knows that. It is recognizing that you need Him because you are not perfect, and God won't let you into heaven unless you can convince Him you are. It just so happens that someone named Jesus paid the price and is the mediator or 'lawyer' for those people that have placed their trust in Him as the one who paid the penalty for their imperfection. In addition, He is there all the time to help you work out your daily problems. Life is a whole lot more fulfilling knowing that you don't have to worry about what happens to you when you die.

"Let's take a few minutes and talk about why some Christians are more effective than others. Remember the story about the sower and the seed? Let's turn to Luke chapter 8 beginning at verse 5.

5 "A sower went out to sow his seed; and as he sowed, some fell by the way side; and it was trodden down, and the fowls of the air devoured it.

6 And some fell upon a rock; and as soon as it was sprung up, it withered away, because it lacked moisture.

7 And some fell among thorns; and the thorns sprang up with it, and choked it.

8 And other fell on good ground, and sprang up, and bare fruit an hundredfold. And when he had said these things, he cried, He that hath ears to hear, let him hear.

9 And his disciples asked him, saying, What might this parable be?

10 And he said, Unto you it is given to know the mysteries of the kingdom of God: but to others in parables; That seeing they might not see, and hearing they might not understand.

11 Now the parable is this; The seed is the Word of God.

12 Those by the way side are they that hear; then cometh the devil; and taketh away the word out of their hearts, lest they should believe and be saved.

13 They on the rock are they, which, when they hear, receive the word with joy; and these have no root, which for a while believe, and in time of temptation fall away.

14 And that which fell amongst thorns are they, which, when they have heard, go forth, and are choked with cares and riches and pleasures of this life, and bring no fruit to perfection.

15 But that on the good ground are they, which in an honest and good heart, having heard the word; keep it, and bring forth fruit with patience.

16 No man, when he lighteth a candle, covereth it with a vessel, or putteth it under a bed; but setteth it on a candlestick, that they which enter in may see the light.

17 For nothing is secret, that shall not be made manifest; neither any thing hid, that shall not be known and come abroad.

18 Take heed therefore how ye hear: for whosoever hath, to him shall be given; and whosoever hath not, from him shall be taken even that which he seemeth to have."

Bob paused for a moment and looked around at everyone which caused Brad to squirm in his seat.

"What do you notice from verse 14? What sort of people can you think of today that are in this category? I'll name a few: Many people are constantly worrying about something. Notice that ... as a rule they will worry a lot and pray little.

"Many people these days are into pleasure. We have more technology now than any other time in history. We have so much in fact that we have much more free time than ever before. What do we do with all this free time? Do we spend more time with God? Not really. In fact we spend less. Most people now fill the void with sports (baseball, soccer, football), entertainment (computers, DVDs, CDs, golf), lewd conduct, shopping, and in general just pleasing ourselves with as much as we can. If we have not kept up with the Joneses, we'll work till we can get what they have, or better yet, we buy it anyway on credit and work to pay for it later. How do you really know that it interferes in the lives of Christians? It is when they can't make church or Sunday school due to one of these activities. I'm not only talking about the ones that are during church time but ones that happen right after (so they miss church), or even better...the activities that are the night before that leave people so tired that they can't drag themselves out of bed to get to church on Sunday.

"As long as we're on this subject, let's talk about work on Sunday. How many people (no need to raise your hand), go to malls or out to eat on Sunday? Have you ever thought that the people that are waiting on you are not going to church because they have to work to serve you? What sort of witness are you providing by going out to eat on Sunday and then not leaving a tip for the waitress and only leaving a tract? Wouldn't it be a better witness to either not go at all, or at least leave a very big tip, a tip so big that the waitress wouldn't have to work the next Sunday and might actually be able to make it to church?

"The last piece of verse 14 discusses riches. Is it a sin to be rich? No! So what's bad about being rich? Nothing except that it is usually an obsession. If a little is good, a lot is even better and even more is better yet. In short, the person is never satisfied, and it is usually a sign that the person only wants more and more and more.

"So how 'bout it, friends? Who'd like to rededicate their lives or for that matter, do it for the first time? How many of you feel you have a hole in your life that needs to be plugged? Only Jesus can do that. You don't have to feel funny, there are a whole lot of people out there that were thought to be believers that never were. It was only when the Holy Spirit touched them that at some point in time (only God knows when and why) that they decided to make a true commitment. So...just come on up, friends, as we have the closing hymn. The deacons and I will pray for you. Our closing hymn will be number 223 *Joyful, Joyful we Adore Thee.* Please stand."

Brad stood up and felt the most confused he had been in his whole life. This pastor wasn't the idiot that he thought most pastors were, he spoke like he had authority. He even seemed to understand science. What was he supposed to do now? He felt like he should do something. Other people were going up to where the pastor was. It looks like the pastor was praying with them. The lady in her twenties also went up. The look in her face seemed to show a real need for something. Brad felt himself being drawn toward the front of the room. He didn't know why other than he realized that the pastor seemed to make sense. Brad didn't know what he'd do when got there other than say hello. He walked out of his pew and up to the pastor.

Brad spoke up first saying, "I'm not sure why I'm here, but I feel like I was drawn up here to speak to you."

Bob, sensing that Brad was led there by the Holy Spirit, decided to lead by saying, "I think the Holy Spirit led you here. You may not know what that means, but I'll pray, and we'll see where it leads us."

Bob took a deep breath and began praying while Brad closed his eyes and stood there listening, "Lord, this man has come here because he feels your Spirit moving within him. Open his mind and his heart to your calling, and bring him the peace that only you can give. I can feel his restlessness and his yearning for you. Please draw him close to you and guide him in the direction that you would have him go. Let him give his heart to Jesus and begin learning about your Word and the truth. Amen."

Bob and Brad opened their eyes, and Brad felt the best he had in a long time.

Bob then spoke to Brad and said, "There are some basic scriptures that you should know."

Brad shook his head and said, "Go ahead."

Bob started off.

"John 3:16 – For God so loved the world, that he gave his only begotten Son, that whosoever believeth in him should not perish, but have everlasting life."

"Romans 3:23 – For all have sinned and fall short of the glory of God."

"Romans 6:23 – For the wages of sin is death; but the gift of God is eternal life through Jesus Christ our Lord."

"Romans 5:8 – But God commendeth his love toward us, in that, while we were yet sinners, Christ died for us."

"First Peter 5:7 – Casting all your care upon him; for he careth for you."

"Ephesians 2:8 and 9 – For by grace are ye saved through faith; and that not of yourselves; it is the gift of God; Not of works, lest any man should boast."

Bob stopped for a minute and then spoke up again.

"I know this is a lot to absorb, but I'll give you a Bible before you leave and some recommended places to start reading."

Brad nodded his head and then turned around. Johnny came up to him and gave him a hug and then Faith ran up and jumped in his arms. Brad gave her a hug and actually started crying.

A thought came into Brad's mind and he spoke to the pastor.

"I feel as though this church is desperately in need of funds. Can you tell me what you need to survive for the moment? Never mind. I'll just write you a check for $50,000. That should cover your expenses till I come back next week."

This took Bob totally by surprise. All Bob could say was, "God bless you, brother."

Chapter 5

The Next Few Months

Brad spent the next week reading the bible that Bob had given him. He was totally absorbed in learning as much as he could about Jesus. Though he had previously only known about some standard bible stories, by the time that the following Sunday rolled around, he had finished the entire New Testament. He particularly found the Gospels fascinating and the issues that the New Testament church faced. Johnny who was the adult Sunday School teacher was amazed at what Brad had learned within a week.

"You've come quite a long way within a week," declared Johnny.

Brad looked at him with a smile and replied, "I'm trying to make up for lost time."

It was about time for church to start and Brad noticed the young woman he saw the previous week who appeared to be hurting, coming into the church. She still appeared to be solemn.

"Johnny, what can you tell about the young woman?"

"Sad story. She lost her husband about six months ago and has seemed lost ever since. It's as if she has totally lost her direction."

"I'm sorry. Do you think there's anything I can do for her?"

Johnny thought for a minute and replied, "I think only God can heal her wounds. Only time will tell."

Faith came out of the Sunday School room and ran toward Brad who picked her up and gave her a hug.

"Will you sit with me again?" Faith asked.

Brad smiled and replied, "Of course I will, Princess."

"Good. I really liked showing you the ropes."

This made everyone in ear shot turn around and smile.

As the service was ending, and Bob gave the altar call, Brad decided it was time to make his public profession of faith and went up to the front of the church where he met Bob. After the two talked for a minute, Bob addressed the congregation.

"Brother Brad has decided to give his life to Christ and has asked to be a member of this congregation. Does the congregation accept Brad as a member of the Greene Community Church? All in favor say aye."

A resounding "Aye" could be heard in the building after which Bob followed it up with, "All opposed, same sign."

Hearing nothing, Bob shook Brad's hand and then gave him a hug.

"Everyone feel free to come up, and welcome Brad to the congregation."

As you might expect, Faith was the first to run up and jump in Brad's arms. He gave her a kiss on the cheek which would have been something that he'd have never done a couple of weeks earlier. Others followed suit including Johnny, Linda, Sue, and other members of the congregation. Finally, the young woman that appeared so solemn came forward and shook Brad's hand.

With a forced smile the young woman said, "Welcome to the family."

Brad realized that she was having troubles and decided to break the ice.

"Thank you. I'm Brad Crawford, and you are Miss..."

"Mrs. Stephanie Morris. My husband passed away 6 months ago today."

Brad wasn't quite sure what to say but with a very concerned look responded with, "I'm terribly sorry. If there's anything I can ever do for you, please don't hesitate to ask."

Stephanie forced a smile and nodded her head, but the tears began to form in her eyes and soon started rolling down her cheeks.

Brad didn't know if this was appropriate but instinctively went forward and put his arms around her and gave her a hug. He realized that in a different setting this might have been wrong, but in the church environment, he was sure it would be fine. When Sue and Linda saw what was happening, they came over and also gave Stephanie a hug.

Over the next several months Brad became more involved with the church and much more knowledgeable about Christian teaching. One particular day in the fall he got an idea that maybe he should get a real choir started at the church though he felt he may need to start with music since Mrs. Juniper was now in a nursing home. An idea suddenly popped into his head.

"Maybe if I get Stephanie more involved in thinking about others by getting her to sing in the choir, maybe she'll start to feel better. It might be risky, but I think I'll chance it."

He found her number in the church directory and then picked up his cell phone and dialed. One ring, two rings, three rings. At last it sounded like the phone was picked up, and the voice on the other end said in an almost sad tone, "Good Morning."

"Stephanie, this is Brad Crawford."

After a few seconds, she replied, "Hello Brad. What can I do for you?"

"Funny you should mention that. I was thinking, since Mrs. Juniper isn't likely coming back to play piano, I was thinking the church could use some music."

After a couple of seconds he continued with, "I'm a pretty decent piano player, and I can also play viola and some trombone."

Stephanie broke in with, "From what I hear in church, you can sing pretty well, too."

Though taken aback, Brad continued. "Well thanks. I don't mind singing while playing the piano but I could use some other accompaniment. Do you think that you could sing along with me? I've heard your voice in church, and I think that we'd make a pretty good pair for the special music time in the service."

Stephanie blushed. After thinking for a second she realized that nobody had given her a real compliment since before her husband had died. She was also glad that Brad couldn't see her now. Strange as it may have seemed, she actually felt good that someone was thinking about her future, and she began to smile. Not a forced one but a real heartfelt smile. With that, she decided to accept the offer.

"I'm not sure how I'd be, but I'd be willing to give it a try."

"Excellent. Do you have plans tonight? I thought that maybe we could practice."

Stephanie's heart began to race as she thought for a second. "I'm free."

"Good. How about if I pick you up at 6 and we'll talk about what to play and sing over dinner. You pick the spot, and I'll treat. After dinner we can go to the church for practice."

Stephanie was speechless and had to think quickly. Was he interested in her, or was he just trying to get some music in the church as he said? Since she really didn't feel threatened, she decided to accept.

"Sounds like fun. I'll be ready at 6. Is there anything that I should bring?"

"Actually, if you could start thinking about some songs or hymns, that would be great."

"I'll do that. Thanks for the invite. I'll be looking forward to it."

"Okay, see you at 6. Goodbye."

"Goodbye, Brad."

After Brad got off the phone all he could say was, "Yes, Yes."

Stephanie got off the phone and took a deep breath. She smiled, stood up and walked over to the mirror in her bedroom. She looked at herself and smiled all the more.

"I have my whole life ahead of me. I think it's about time I started acting like it."

With that she went to her wardrobe and stared pulling out clothes that might be attractive but modest. Though she was a little nervous, she started feeling more confident than she had in a long time.

"Ah, this dress should be perfect. Now for some earrings, a nice necklace with a cross, a little perfume, and voila. A new me!"

Brad arrived at her house promptly at 6 and knocked on her front door.

Though she shouldn't have been surprised, the knock startled Stephanie, and her heart almost skipped a beat. As she took a deep breath before answering the door, she said to herself, "Okay, calm down." After a few seconds of hesitation, she became more confident, smiled and said, "It's time to get this show on the road."

With that, she went to the door, opened it, and gave Brad a warm smile. Brad took one look at her and almost fell over with amazement. She looked beautiful. No, she looked gorgeous. Was this the same Stephanie that he had seen in church? Was that one call to her all it took to change her this much?

Seeing that Brad appeared speechless made Stephanie smile all the more. With that, she managed to get up enough courage to talk. "Would you like to come in for a minute?" she asked.

Once he got over the shock, he shook his head in the affirmative and walked in. Stephanie had a modest home but well cared for.

"All I need to do is get on my shoes and coat and I'll be ready," she said.

With that she left the room and was back in less than a minute.

"Okay, all set."

With that Brad opened the door, locked it from the inside, and closed it once he and Stephanie walked out. "Do you have any preference on dinner?" he asked.

"If you like German, there's a local restaurant that is excellent," she said.

"That works for me. I have seen it on the way down to church but I've never been there," he replied satisfied that she had actually picked out something she might like.

They continued to have small talk as they traveled to the restaurant, but their real discussion began after they finished ordering.

"Before we get down to business, tell me a little about yourself," he asked.

Stephanie didn't quite know where to begin. This was all so new to her. She hadn't really been on a date in a while and wasn't quite sure where to begin, though somehow she actually felt comfortable with Brad.

"I grew up around Stanardsville, went to high school with my late husband, and we were real high school sweethearts. I then went to college at UVA." With that she began to think about the fun times she had with her late husband and almost started to cry but then shook her head to stop herself from breaking down and was about to continue when Brad interrupted and stretched out his hand across the table and held hers in a real comforting way.

"I'm sorry, let's try another subject," he said trying his best to distract her. "For the entire time I've been at the church, I've noticed that Sunday attendance is only about 20 people including the pastor. I think I've helped to stabilize the budget, but we need more people. From what you have seen in the past, is there much change around Christmas?"

This seemed to get Stephanie to concentrate on something else and calm down. She pondered this for a second and then spoke up. "From what I've seen there isn't much change at all."

With a determined look, Brad said, "then it's about time we do something about it. We need something to draw people in. Music would definitely help, which is where you and I come in, but I think we need something more and Christmas seems like the most convenient time to draw people to the church."

Brad took a breath before he continued. "I've got a thought and I'd like to run it by you." Brad smiled and said "Promise not to laugh," he said with a raised eyebrow and a shaking index finger.

Stephanie looked at him rather puzzled but shook her head in the affirmative.

"Good," Brad indicated. "Here's my plan. I have some connections with Starr Carpenter, also known as Starr Gazer. She and I met once at a conference about a year ago. She doesn't know that I'm Christian, and I expect I can use that to our advantage. I think she would be willing to help us with our church attendance problems."

Stephanie looked rather puzzled and asked, "What can she do?"

"That's the interesting part. I believe that she can time warp. I'm going to ask her to film the time around Jesus' birth (e.g. birth, angels, shepherds) in a 360 degree by 360 degree high definition format and bring back the recording. I'll then set up projection equipment in the church and advertise the entire thing as an Extreme Christmas. The newspapers will eat this up since it's got both Starr and myself as the ones promoting the event."

"What makes you think that Starr will go along with it?" she asked.

"It's just a hunch. I'll think about calling her tomorrow. For now, how 'bout if we concentrate on the hymns we'll sing together for the service on Sunday? Do you have anything particularly in mind for special music?"

Stephanie thought for a moment and said, "Yes, how about *The Church in the Wildwood* and *Give Me Oil in my Lamp*? They're both lively and...truthfully...I believe that the church could use a little liveliness."

Brad smiled and said, "That'll work and I can even liven up the piano playing a little to make everyone stomp their feet."

This made Stephanie smile.

Once they had eaten and left the restaurant, they went to church to practice for about half an hour and Brad took Stephanie home. Once Stephanie went in the house and closed the door, she closed her eyes and breathed a sigh of relief. She honestly had a good time and actually liked Brad. He seemed like a nice man and she hoped he'd ask her out on a real date, although this seemed as close to a date as she'd had in a long time. It was about 9:00 by this time and she decided to do some Bible reading and then get ready for bed.

When Brad left Stephanie's house he breathed a sigh of relief but just made a fist and pulled his arm in a downward motion and said, "Yes!"

The next day he found his notes from the conference where he met Starr and finding her phone number decided to give her a call. Jennifer answered the phone.

"Hello, Carpenter residence."

"Hello, this is Brad Crawford from Crawford Enterprises. May I speak to Starr, please?"

"Yes, Mr. Crawford. She's in the lab working with her father. It'll take a minute to get her; can you hold?"

"Yes, ma'am."

A minute later, Starr picked up the phone and said, "Hello, this is Starr."

"Hello Starr, this is Brad Crawford. I met you at a conference a few months ago."

Starr seemed a little apprehensive since she remembered Brad as a very shallow, egotistical man. She didn't know what he wanted, so she decided to be rather cautious.

"Yes, I remember you, Mr. Crawford. What can I do for you?"

"I've become a Christian in the last few months and I'm attending a small church in the Greene County area in Virginia. There is very low attendance, and I thought of an idea for increasing attendance and getting some more publicity for the overall church of Christ."

As he took a breather, Starr breathed a sigh of relief herself since Brad seemed closer to a normal human being than she remembered. After he inhaled, he continued with his request.

"I believe that what we need to get people to come to the gospel is to get them to see it first-hand. I thought that a 3D 360 by 360 degree projection of the angels, shepherds and the birth in the stable could be a good witness. I could set up the projection equipment, but I could use someone to go back in time to collect the video and audio. I was hoping that would be you."

Starr was caught totally off guard but said, "You're hoping to produce a *Thomas* effect perhaps?"

"That could be one way to look at it," he replied.

"You realize that God wants people to believe without having to see first-hand, don't you?"

"Yes, but if that's the only way people believe, that's probably better than being lost forever, don't you think?"

"Let me talk to my parents, and I'll be in touch. By the way, where is this church and when are the services?"

Brad gave Starr the directions and the time of the service, and then they said goodbye.

It was still a couple of days before Sunday so Brad took advantage of the time and practiced with Stephanie as often as he could. This was partially due to actually needing the practice and also due to his interest in Stephanie. Now Stephanie was also developing some interest in Brad by this time and eagerly waited for the times that he would call or they would be together. Sunday morning came and just before the service began, in walked Starr and her family. As Brad saw them, he walked over to say hello. He motioned to Stephanie to come over as well.

"Hello, Starr, I'm glad to see you. This is my friend, Stephanie. We're going to attempt to sing some special music together a little later in the service."

"Glad to meet you," Starr said to Stephanie. "This is my family, mom, dad, and my brothers, Andrew and Luke."

"Glad to meet you, too," replied Stephanie and Brad almost simultaneously.

Brad spoke up saying, "We can talk later, but I need to get to the piano to begin the prelude."

Brad and Stephanie excused themselves while the Carpenter family found themselves a seat. The service was very well done, and the congregation was excited about having a new piano player, nice vocalists and some excellent special music.

Once the service was over, Brad and Stephanie walked over to Starr along with the pastor, Sue, Johnny and Linda. Brad made the introductions, and Bob seemed quite taken aback at having such high profile people in his little country church.

"Dad and I talked it over, and we agreed to help you out. What type of equipment do you need me to bring back to the past with me?" asked Starr.

"I'll get you everything you need tomorrow morning. I'll work on the projection equipment while you get everything recorded," replied Brad.

This just made Starr laugh. "I can tell you aren't used to time travel Mr. Crawford. I'll be back with the recordings virtually immediately after I leave you. If you would have had the equipment with you now, I'd probably already be done."

Brad thought for a minute and realized that Starr was correct. "I hadn't thought about it that way." Brad wasn't used to dealing with people of the caliber of Starr and Matthew. He would enjoy talking to them more on a technical level when he had the chance.

Stephanie had thought of inviting Brad, the Tanners and the Taylors to dinner at her place after church and thought she may as well invite the Carpenters over as well.

"Would you all like to come over for lunch? I have Brunswick stew cooking in the crock pot and also had some bread that should be ready to put in the oven. I had also made a German chocolate cake. There should be enough for everyone."

Matthew and Jennifer thought it would be a good idea to get to know the people of the area, and the Taylors and Tanners were happy to see Stephanie so hospitable that they just accepted by default. Brad looked at Stephanie and winked. Stephanie took that as a yes.

The group carpooled over to Stephanie's since the Carpenters didn't drive to the church but transported via Starr. Stephanie had everything close to prepared, and it wasn't long before dinner was ready.

Starr and Matthew wanted to probe Brad in order to find out a little more about his sudden transformation. Matthew decided to bring it up. "So Brad, tell me about your ministry here at the church and your salvation experience?"

Brad seemed a little taken aback but started talking about how he was physically saved by Johnny and then how Pastor Bob's sermon had an effect on him. The answers seemed to be satisfactory enough for Matthew and Starr to feel encouraged.

When lunch was over the Carpenters decided to excuse themselves.

"Thank you so much for your hospitality, but we probably need to get going," Matthew said as he looked at his watch.

Starr looked at Brad and said, "Give me a call at home as soon as you're ready and I'll transport to your location."

"That'll be fine," responded Brad.

With that Starr thought for a second and said, "Don't be alarmed but I'm going to transform, and there'll be a bright flash."

The newbies shook their heads, and then Starr transformed. A few seconds later she and her family disappeared.

Brad was very impressed, though the other folks just sat there stunned.

The next morning Brad finished the equipment that Starr would need to take with her. He then decided to call her.

"Starr, this is Brad. I have everything ready so when you're set, you can…" Brad stopped talking when he saw a bright flash of light in his office. He then hung up the phone and looked at Starr with a smile and a nod. He continued his conversation with, "That's pretty impressive. Okay, I guess I should show you how this equipment works."

Starr paid careful attention and shook her head indicating that she understood. She looked at Brad and said, "I decided to travel back to the right time and locate everything including the right stable and the location of the shepherds. I thought that would save me some effort later since I wouldn't have to lug around any equipment while looking for everything."

"You mean you've already been there and seen everything?"

"That's right. It pretty well confirmed everything I already knew," replied Starr.

Starr showed Brad some of the footage she had already taken. He was very impressed and just said, "I'm sure that you'll know what the right amount of footage will be. We'll need enough for about a couple of hours after edits."

"That's about what I would have thought. Okay, I'm ready to go."

Starr took the equipment and said goodbye. With that, a bright flash appeared, and almost immediately, a second flash appeared and Starr was back.

"Wow," declared Brad. "That brings new meaning to the term *back in a flash.*"

Starr gave back the equipment and was about to say something when the door opened and Evelyn walked in. She took one look at Starr and screamed.

"It's alright Miss Markham," said Brad. "This is Starr Carpenter, alias Starr Gazer. She's here helping me with a church project."

"Hello," said Starr. "I was just completing my work with Mr. Crawford."

Turning to Brad, Starr said, "If you have any problems, just contact me."

She was just about to say something else when her watch phone rang.

"This is Starr," she said.

The voice on the other end could be heard saying, "This is Agent Thompson. The president needs to see you immediately. There's a problem in Afghanistan, and he needs your assistance ASAP."

"Understood. Be there in a few minutes," she replied.

Starr looked at Evelyn and Brad and said, "Sorry, duty calls. If you need anything, call."

With that, Starr disappeared in a flash.

Brad just smiled, looked at Evelyn and said, "She's something else, isn't she?"

Evelyn just looked amazed and replied, "Yes sir."

It took Brad the better part of a week to view the recordings and edit them. He then spent the next few days setting up the church for a proper viewing including getting all the projection equipment set up as well as getting the proper backgrounds to show it in 360 degree by 360 degree mode. He then called Bob, Johnny, and Stephanie to set a time for a private viewing. He also called Starr and Matthew in case they wanted to come.

As it was now after Thanksgiving, the time would be perfect to have a press conference and begin the nightly public viewings. Brad picked Stephanie up at 6PM to bring her to the viewing. As they approached the church, the other participants were waiting for them in the vestibule.

"Hello, everyone," said Brad with a smile. "If you will all come in to the sanctuary, I'll begin the presentation."

The group went into the sanctuary and were blown away by the amount of equipment that was there. Brad had previously taken the pews out and replaced them with wooden stools in order to enhance the effect and cut down on the impact the pews would have made on the lighting.

"Welcome, everyone," announced Brad. "The Greene Community Church proudly presents the story of Christmas. This is no ordinary Christmas pageant. You might call it an Xtreme Christmas. This presentation is a 360 degree by 360 degree high definition multimedia presentation using audio and video recordings gathered over 2000 years ago. This was made possible through the efforts of Starr Carpenter as she went back to the past and gathered the recordings that we shall now see. Though you will hear the audio in the original languages, an English translation has been made and can be heard via the headphones that you have under your seats. The headphones are cordless, so all you have to do is adjust the volume. Those people that understand the native languages are welcome to listen without the headphones. Now please sit back and relax as you visit the real Mary, Joseph, Jesus, shepherds, angels, and hosts of other people in the real story of Christmas."

The lights dimmed and what everyone saw next were buildings, sand, and hordes of people. The census in Bethlehem was taking place. As the presentation took place, the audience was shown Mary and Joseph looking for a room and eventually finding refuge in a place where the animals were kept near an inn toward the far edge of town. The audience was shown and heard the labor and birth of Jesus (discretely), and the glory of the shepherds and the angels. Lastly, the audience was shown the visit by the wise men from the east, though the time frame was not until after the census was over and Mary, Joseph and Jesus were staying in a house.

"Thank you all for being here tonight," announced Brad. "We hope this has enriched your life and that this will be a Merry and Holy Christmas season for you all. Goodnight."

Everyone clapped and each of the people in church was very impressed.

"Looks like there isn't a dry eye in the house, Brad. Thanks," remarked Bob. Bob then proceeded to give Brad a hug.

When that was over, Brad looked at Starr.

"Would you be willing to get a TV interview with Bob and myself sometime tomorrow?" he asked. "I can probably arrange it with the local NBC affiliate. They'd love the scoop. We'd have it here and would have a showing at the same time."

"I'll probably ask our North Carolina reporter if he'd like to come along," replied Starr.

"That would be fine," he said, nodding his head in an approving manner.

After Starr and her family left, as well as Bob and his family and Johnny and Linda, Brad took Stephanie home. As he dropped her off at her door, she gave him a hug and a kiss on the cheek.

"Thanks," she said. "This was really wonderful. I can't wait till tomorrow when the reporters see this."

Brad was taken aback at the affection but said, "You're welcome. I think it'll be 'jest' fine."

The next day Starr asked the reporter she knew in North Carolina if he'd like to be one of the reporters that would take part in the historic occasion.

"I'd be thrilled," he replied. "Can I bring my camera man with me?"

"Yes of course. I'll transport both of you to Virginia this afternoon at 5pm. Is that okay?"

"That'll be a story all by itself. We'll be ready...and thanks."

"Great. I'll be at your office ready to pick you up a few minutes to 5. Goodbye".

Starr worked with her father on one of her many projects till it was time to go and then transported to the office of the reporter. Starr found them ready, and the three of them transported to the small Virginia church.

"Wow," exclaimed the reporter. "That was the wildest feeling I've ever had. This trip will have been worth it just for that."

"Glad you enjoyed it," replied Starr. "Now let's get to work."

The camera man set up his equipment, and the reporter was introduced to Brad and the pastor. The reporter had heard a lot about Brad and Crawford Enterprises and took careful notes. The local Virginia TV affiliate was just arriving, and the reporter and camera man felt lucky that they were there first. The interview they had with Brad and the pastor had already been transmitted to their newspaper and was going to the Associated Press (AP) wire. The second part of the news story was about to begin.

Brad and Pastor Bob got up in front of the audience which included the news reporters, camera men, some local politicians and some local clergy.

Bob gave an introduction, and then Brad gave his welcome and his explanation of the technology. As the pageant took place, the audience had expressions showing tears, and many vocal expressions of amazement and wonder. When the pageant was complete, clapping could be heard from everyone in attendance including all the reporters and cameramen. Note that since this was being recorded and transmitted live to many television stations, many people could see it at the same time.

Once the clapping subsided, Brad spoke up saying, "Thank you all for attending. For those people in the television audience that want to come see this first hand, there will be a showing every night at 7PM from tomorrow night through January 6th. Anyone interested in knowing more about the Gospel can talk to Pastor Bob at any time. Goodnight."

Once Brad finished, the reporters could be heard in front of their cameras making their final comments and signing off. Starr transported herself and the reporter and cameraman back to North Carolina.

Bob thanked Brad for all his hard work, and then Bob's family and Johnny's family left for the night.

Brad then looked at Stephanie and breathed a sigh of relief. She responded, with "I know what you mean."

"Are you ready to go home?" asked Brad.

"Yup. I could use a good night's sleep", she responded.

Brad drove Stephanie home and then before she got out of the car, asked her, "I know you're going to think me a little forward, but I feel like we've grown rather close in the last number of months. You don't have to give me an answer now, but," Brad took a deep breath and finished with, "would you marry me?"

Stephanie smiled and responded with, "I don't have to think it over. Yes, I was hoping you'd ask me. I haven't felt this way in a long time."

With that she leaned over and kissed him.

Part II

Typical Starr Adventures

Chapter 6

A Case of Anonymity

"Hey dad," an excited Starr shouted. "Here's an ad in *U.S. Christian* Magazine for a work and evangelism trip to Bolivia for fifteen to nineteen year old students in a couple of months over Christmas break. I'd really like to go, but I'm afraid that people will recognize me by name and I'll be hounded the whole trip. What's the chance that I could keep my identity a secret?"

Starr was 17 years old and quite mature for her age. Her formal education had been recently completed as she had graduated from Waynesport Christian High School. That had been her education for "social skills" and not for normal formal learning. She had numerous Bachelor, Masters and Doctoral degrees in rather technical subjects and had been employed by the Federal Government on an as needed basis for years as Starr Gazer. Her father, Matthew, was busy along with her mother, Jennifer, and her brothers, Andrew and Luke (who was still 2 years old). Matthew was still inventing and was always busy doing something. The term *always* was truer than you think since neither he nor Starr needed sleep. Starr had been dating her boyfriend Jeff for a few years already, and it seemed like forever to her.

Her dad thought for a moment and spoke up saying, "I expect that Agent Thompson can come up with some papers that could easily help you with that. Why don't you ask him?"

"Sounds like a good idea. I'll call him this afternoon," she said.

By afternoon, Starr had asked for some motherly advice from her mother about Jeff and whether she needed any babysitting in the foreseeable future. Starr then decided it was about time to talk to Agent Thompson, and so she placed the call.

"Agent Thompson, this is Starr."

"Hello, Starr. What can I do for my favorite superhero today?"

With a little sarcasm in her voice she replied, "Now how many superheroes do you know?"

"Counting you, that's one. In any case, what can I do for you?"

"With all of my adventures, it's hard for me to keep my identity a secret when I just want to go places for fun. Is there any chance I can get a new identity for times I want to take a trip? To make a long story short, I'm interested in going on a work and evangelism trip to Bolivia but would like to keep my identity a secret. I would really like to go and not feel hounded as Starr Gazer."

Agent Thompson thought for a couple of seconds and said, "I don't think it would be much of a problem. I can probably get you a social security number, birth certificate, and a driver's license by tomorrow. Is that soon enough?"

"That's plenty quick. Do you have any idea what sort of name might be appropriate?"

"If this were a true covert operation, I'd have a different opinion but I'd say just use your middle name and maybe your mother's maiden name."

"Ok, that would make it Elizabeth Tucker. Great, now I can submit my application for the trip. Is there any other information you need from me?"

"Yes. How about an address?"

"We'll use my grandmother's address. I think you have that, don't you?"

"Yes, I do. That should be sufficient. Since it's not a total rush, I should get it all by tomorrow and ship it to you overnight."

"That's excellent. I'll be looking forward to it. Thank you so much, sir."

"Glad I could be of service to you for once. Good bye Starr...I mean Elizabeth."

Starr laughed and then said, "Goodbye, sir."

While she was waiting for her new identity papers that she was to receive two days later, she went on-line and registered for the trip. She almost forgot to put her new name and address.

"I'll need to remind myself a little more often to respond to the name Elizabeth Tucker. Maybe I can get mom and dad to help me in that department."

As the weeks passed, Starr worked on other cases with Agent Thompson and had her usual dates with Jeff. Finally, the day came for her to leave. They were all to meet at Dulles airport in Virginia at the main terminal since they would need to transfer to the international terminal before departure. Starr had no trouble using her new identification to get on the plane going to

Dulles. Agent Thompson had done his job well. Upon arrival at Dulles, Starr went from terminal C to the main terminal and got her luggage for the trip to Bolivia. It was not an automatic transfer. Once she had her luggage, she walked up the escalator to the check-in point. She knew she was in the right place when she saw a sign saying, *Bolivian Work Trip* with a fish symbol. She saw a man and woman that looked like they could have been in charge and walked up to them.

"Hello, I'm Elizabeth Tucker."

The woman smiled and said, "Hello Elizabeth. I'm Christine Wallace and this is my husband George. The other children have all arrived and are standing over by the window looking at planes. This should be a good trip. There are an exact number of boys and girls. Ten apiece. This is the first time we've had that perfect a split before."

"I think I'll wander over to meet them," said Starr.

"We should be checking in within the next half hour so we'll come get you when we're ready," said Mr. Wallace.

Starr wandered over to the group and introduced herself.

"Hi, I'm Elizabeth. I came in from North Carolina."

Each of the young adults introduced themselves and Starr took careful note of their names as well as their mannerisms. One girl named Kristy seemed particularly shy and Starr thought it would be good for the girl to seem like she had a friend so she decided to strike up a conversation and see where it led.

"Have you ever been on one of these type of trips before?" asked Starr.

Kristy eyed Starr for a second and then with a sigh said, "No. This was another bright idea of my parents to get me out of the house and mingle with other people. They thought that if I had a hard time to talk to people in America that maybe I'd have better luck in a foreign country. At least my Spanish is very good."

Starr was taken aback but quickly recovered and smiling, said, "Well, I have no problem if you hang out with me."

By that time the Wallaces came over and collecting the group of teenagers managed to help them get through the boarding process. The plane was a 777 and thus there were seats in the middle as well as sides. Starr sat next to a girl named Becky, a real talker. Starr could already tell it was going to be a long flight from Washington to Cochabamba, Bolivia. Before Starr knew it, she knew much more about Becky than she ever wanted to know. Since Starr didn't need to sleep, she had to wait for Becky to talk herself out and eventually drift off to sleep. Even though Starr did some reading to keep from being totally bored, she still had plenty of time. She decided to close her eyes once in a while just to make it appear as though she was sleeping.

Eventually the plane landed and the passengers disembarked. Mr. and Mrs. Wallace gathered their little troop and found the bus driver that would take them as far as he could. They all entered the bus which was like an old school bus and the group finally realized how much the climate had changed.

Becky was one of the first to complain, "Is it going to be this hot the whole trip? This bus doesn't have any air conditioning, does it?"

Mr. Wallace smiled and answered, "Answer to question one: Quite likely. Answer to question two: It doesn't."

Becky shook her head and sighed, "It couldn't hurt to ask."

It was definitely hot and humid. The native people didn't seem to mind at all, not much different than Eskimos living in the far north or the bush men of Africa. Once people are taken out of their native habitat, they don't do as well.

The trip from the airport to their work site was several hours long and since it was the middle of the day and close to the equator, the heat was very noticeable. The crew complained but survived. At last they came to the end of their bus trip. The bus driver stopped at the end of the road, as there was no more road. As Mr. Wallace asked the bus driver what was supposed to happen now, a couple of men appeared from a small trail just in front of the bus. Mr. Wallace got out and talked to the men and then came back to the bus.

"Okay, everyone. We have to walk from here. It's about 2500 meters from here to the little village that needs our help. Remember that we're here to help after the earthquake, and these people may not have seen too many white people. Let's give them a good impression of America and show our faith."

The teens groaned but got off the bus and got their belongings for the hike to the village.

Starr thought this to be a rather interesting adventure and was amused at the other teens. They all walked single file along some rather rough terrain. They were traveling about 10 meters apart and were not making very good time due to the loads they were carrying. Becky complained as usual, and Starr simply smiled. They came to a rocky overhang and passed underneath single file. Becky heard something odd and as she turned, she just froze and screamed.

One of the guides rushed up and realized what the problem was. "Stay back everyone. This is a very poisonous snake, it is a type of pit viper."

Now the snake was quite jumpy and had Becky cornered. When Starr arrived she surveyed the situation and noticed the machete that the guide had. She realized that if she timed it just right, she could grab the machete and surprise the snake from the back and catch it just behind the head.

"Excuse me sir," declared Starr as she extracted the machete from the guide's sheath. "I need to borrow this for a minute."

With that, she whipped the machete around like a martial arts person would do with a sword in order to test the feel of the weapon and then sprung forward bringing the sharpest portion of the machete down on the back of the head of the snake. This virtually severed the head from the rest of the body. Becky screamed as the snake twisted and turned, though it was quite dead. Everyone but Starr was in a state of shock, since for her, it was just routine.

The boys were very impressed and nodded their heads in a very approving manner. One of them named Brad asked, "Where'd you learn to do that, Elizabeth?"

Starr looked at him and said, "I'm a sixth degree black belt."

Brad was shocked but smiling said, "I certainly won't mess with you."

Once the group calmed down, they continued along their journey to the village. Upon arrival, they saw the destruction from the earthquake. There were only a few of the huts rebuilt, and it appeared like there were at least two dozen that were in shambles. Everyone but Starr and the Wallaces were a little shocked at the clothes that the natives wore. As would be standard for a hot climate, they were scantily dressed.

Starr looked around at the broken buildings and said to herself, "Looks like we've got some work to do. I don't know how many of these kids are really up to the work. The girls seem pretty squeamish."

As it was late afternoon, the group thought it would be a good idea to work on setting up their tents for the night. The women and girls of the village were about to prepare supper so Mrs. Wallace and some of the work crew girls decided to help them. Mr. Wallace and the work crew boys dealt with getting the tents set up. Starr decided to survey the quake damage and get a feel for how to proceed in the morning. Her Spanish was very good even without the universal translator that came with the Starr Gazer suit so she decided to talk to one of the natives.

"How have you been proceeding when rebuilding these huts? What sort of tools have you been using?"

The native man named Jose looked at her for a minute with a curious look but then explained, "We have been using these tools here."

There were some crude hammers, some old style saws, some hatchets, and some machetes.

"No wonder it's taking so long to rebuild," Starr thought to herself. "We have a few tools with us but we don't have near enough to be of any major help. I could get some in a flash but that would defeat the purpose of my being anonymous here. It would seem pretty strange for tools to just automatically appear."

Starr rejoined the group as supper was just about ready. Supper consisted of some native fruits and vegetables as well as roasted wild boar.

"This should be a great meal," said Starr to the group. "I haven't tasted these fruits before. I believe that they can't grow in the States and they can't be transported to us due to their short shelf life after picking."

"That's correct," replied Mrs. Wallace. "We should get to experience a lot of varied tastes while we're here."

One boy named Billy exclaimed, "And probably a whole lot of unplanned disasters as well."

For the primitive area that they were in, the food was really quite good. The boar could have used a little marinating or at least some barbecue sauce.

Once supper was over, the group helped to clean up, and Mr. Wallace sat everyone down to tell a Bible story around the fire. Once the story was done, it was time for bed. Starr decided to pair up with Kristy in a small pup tent. This would allow them to talk some more.

"Come on, Kristy, our tent is over here," said Starr.

Kristy was starting to feel a little scared, and Starr had to calm her down. Once they were bedded down for the night, Kristy's paranoia started kicking in with all the strange jungle sounds.

"What was that?" Kristy said jumping up as a predatory cat was heard in the distance.

"Sounds about like a jaguar," replied Starr.

"How do you know so much about the jungle, Elizabeth?" asked Kristy.

"I read a lot."

"There's something strange about you, Elizabeth. I haven't quite put my finger on it yet, but I will."

"You're a funny one, Kristy. You seem to be suspicious of everything. Sometimes you just have to accept things the way they are. Didn't you accept Jesus that way?"

Kristy thought for a minute and then said, "I guess you're right. Thanks, Elizabeth."

"You're welcome. Good night Kristy."

Starr was obviously not sleepy but relaxed while listening to the jungle sounds. She said some prayers and just lay there and enjoyed the jungle music. About half way into the night, Starr heard one of the cats get a little closer than she'd have expected.

From the sound of it, she'd have guessed no more than 100 yards. She heard some of the village men start moving around and decided to get up and investigate. Luckily she brought a long life flashlight with her with several sets of extra batteries.

When Starr got out of her tent she saw the jaguar to her right about 100 feet away and the men to her left about 50 feet away. The men seemed pretty scared as they didn't have anything in their hands other than a couple of spears. Then Starr remembered the hatchets. They were about 15 feet away to her right. She shined the flashlight toward the location of the hatchets and inched her way to them.

The men of the village yelled out for Starr to stop but Starr had a good idea what to do. Once she got to the hatchets, she picked up two of them, one in each hand while still holding the flashlight in the left hand. She approached the cat who had been approaching the men until it saw Starr. It then focused its attention on her. She was now within about twenty feet of it and had the hatchet in her right hand all balanced and ready to throw. As the cat leaped at her she threw the hatchet which hit the cat directly in the middle of the head, dropping it to the ground. Starr took the other hatchet and cut the throat of the jaguar in one blow.

By this time the entire camp was up, and the men of the village had made it to Starr. They were still afraid of the big cat, though it was quite dead.

One of the men of the village spoke to Starr. "This jaguar has been hurting our people for a long time. He would take some of the children when they wandered off. This has been the first time that he has been this bold and come into the village. You have been a big help to us. Now our village will be safe. Gracias."

"You're very welcome," replied Starr.

The rest of the work campers were up by now and flashed their lights all over the place. Mr. Wallace looked at Starr for a second and asked her aside.

"Elizabeth, you're a brave young girl. Thanks. We'll talk some more in the morning."

"Just trying to help out, sir."

Starr went back to bed with Kristy who looked at her with a rather odd look.

"I still think there's more to you than meets the eye, Elizabeth. By the way – Can I call you Beth?"

Starr thought this was good progress for the shy girl and replied, "Sure Kristy. That would be fine. I've been called worse."

That actually made Kristy laugh which made Starr laugh as well. Starr gave Kristy a hug and said goodnight for the second time.

As the days passed, the group worked on rebuilding the village with the tools they had. It was very hard work, but everyone thought it was worth the effort. The villagers were very grateful and always provided good food for the meals.

The day before they were about to leave, just about dawn, a lot of commotion was heard outside the tents, and then Starr heard some machine gun fire and a lot of shouting.

"This doesn't sound good," Starr said to herself. "These people don't have guns."

Kristy had gone out to the bathroom (which was really an outhouse), so Starr didn't have to worry about her being around. Starr peaked out of the tent and saw six men with guns pointing them at the Wallaces and the work crew. The villagers were screaming and ran off in the woods.

One of the gunmen said in a loud voice, "Don't worry about those village idiots. They won't do anything. We're looking for these Americans. They'll fetch a high price from their government."

He pointed to the other gunmen and said, "Go check the other tents. We want all of them."

The gunmen started pulling the other kids out of their tents and were getting close to Starr's tent.

Starr sighed and said, "I was hoping to avoid this but maybe with a little Starr Gazer trickery I can preserve my anonymity anyway."

With that she said, "Starr power, activate."

After her transformation she said, "Invisibility mode on. Force field on. Set weapons to heavy stun. Transport to ten meters straight up."

With that, she disappeared and moved outside the tent into the air, but invisible. She surveyed the situation and realized that all six gunmen could be seen and clear shots could be taken. Just before one of the gunmen opened her tent, she opened fire and stunned him. Stunning the other gunmen only took another few seconds. Once Starr realized they were out cold, she transported back to her tent and deactivated. She then got out of her tent, and realizing that the other workers were still too scared to do anything, she found some twine and tied up the gunmen taking all their weapons.

The villagers started reappearing, and one of them said that he would travel to a neighboring village and get some help.

Starr looked at the Wallaces and other workers and smiled saying. "I think that should hold them till we get some help."

Everyone gave a sigh of relief, and in a few hours some local police arrived by horseback. The gunmen started to awaken, and the head gunman spoke to the police.

"I don't know what happened. We had everything planned perfectly. It should have been a perfect kidnapping."

The police took the gunmen away, and Mr. Wallace came over to Starr.

"Come over here for a second will you, Elizabeth?"

"Sure Mr. Wallace. What can I do for you?"

After they went off about a hundred feet away from everyone else, Mr. Wallace looked at Starr and said, "I somehow have a feeling you had something to do with capturing those men. I'm not sure how, but I just thought I'd say thanks anyway."

"I'm not really sure what you mean, but I'm always willing to take a compliment."

Starr tried to hide her smile but couldn't quite pull it off.

Mr. Wallace picked up on it and just winked at her.

"By the way Mr. Wallace, it's Epiphany. So...just in case I didn't say it earlier this trip, Happy New Year and a belated Merry Christmas."

"Happy New Year to you too, Starr."

The rest of the trip was uneventful, and Starr made it back home safely. As soon as her father saw Starr he asked, "I noticed the suit was activated once. So what happened?"

Starr smiled and said, "No big deal dad. Just a routine work trip in the jungle."

Matthew knew better and just shook his head and laughed.

Chapter 7

A Request from the President

It was a few weeks before Christmas, and Jennifer Carpenter had just finished making breakfast for the family. As they were sitting down to eat she looked at her son, Luke, in a stern manner. He was only two years old and tried to get away with anything he could.

"Now I expect you to eat all of your breakfast. Do you understand me?" she asked.

He looked her in a very defiant way but just said, "Yes, mommy."

Just as she was about to say something else, the phone rang. Everyone at the table looked at each other, and then Matthew decided to take the call. He picked it up on the fourth ring.

"Hello, this is Matthew Carpenter."

"Hello, Dr. Carpenter. This is Agent Thompson. I need to make this short, but the President would like to talk to you and Starr at your earliest convenience. Can you be at the White

House this afternoon at 2PM for a meeting with the President, the Secretary of the Defense and the Surgeon General?"

"You do realize that we're in North Carolina, right?"

"Yes but I figured you and Starr could just teleport here like Starr does all the time. We'd like you all to make a rather dramatic entrance anyway, so as to impress the brass."

Matthew looked at Starr and replied, "Just tell us where you want us and we'll be there."

"Good. Show up at the White House door at the Pennsylvania Avenue Entrance at 2PM, and we'll be there."

"Can you tell us what this is about?"

"No...I'd like to let the President do that. Don't worry though, none of them should bite."

"Okay, we'll see you then. Goodbye."

"Goodbye, Matthew."

Matthew looked at his family and then specifically at Starr. Did you hear much of that?

Starr nodded in the affirmative. "Looks like we'll just have to wait and see," she said.

Two o'clock came quickly as there were always plenty of things to do around the Carpenter household. Starr transformed about 1:55 P.M., and then she and her father transported to the White House using a combined transport mechanism that they had not yet fully tested. Usually Starr would transport alone, or she could make others transport, but she had not transported with someone in tow.

When they appeared in front of the White House, Agent Thompson, the President, the Surgeon General, and the Secretary of Defense were there to greet them.

"Hello, Agent Thompson," said Starr. "Is there any need for me to stay in my suit or can I transform back to just being me?"

"It's fine to change back now," replied Agent Thompson.

With that she said, "Starr power, deactivate."

A brilliant flash of light all but blinded the people in the area. By the time the light dissipated, Starr appeared in her regular clothes. She did remember to at least wear something professional. She didn't really have many clothes for a high level business meeting, but she did have a nice blue business suit and a matching blouse. Her mother would not have let her out of the house without looking decent for the President.

After the standard pleasantries Starr and her father were led to a room that was larger than their house. There was a large table in the middle of the room surrounded by lots of chairs, and the entire room had chairs along the walls. There were also a couple of guards at the door entrance.

Once they sat down, the President began to explain the background for why Starr and Matthew had been asked to come to the White House. "History has shown that on the front lines, the lack of a proper diagnosis is the major cause of permanent damage among our soldiers. I understand that the power draw of your *healing machine* is more than we have at the front line mobile hospitals. Dr. Carpenter and Starr, we'd like you think of a way to help diagnose our wounded troops quicker so the repairs could be correct and more efficient."

The Surgeon General spoke up saying, "I have no doubt that you can accomplish the task we have set before you. The current crisis in the Middle East is compounded by the harsh conditions."

"We know that casualties are a fact of life in war situations, but we'd like to think that we could cut down on the permanent damage that soldiers have to deal with once they get home," included the Secretary of Defense.

The President spoke back up. "So you see, we think that you people are the only ones that have a chance of helping our troops have a productive life when they get back home."

Matthew looked at Starr and then nodded his head saying, "I don't see much problem with getting a diagnostic machine to the front lines within a week or so."

"That fast?" replied the President.

"Yes sir," replied Matthew. "Not much of a problem. You just tell us where to be, and we'll get ourselves there. If we could get some papers that would identify us and maybe call ahead to the surgical unit so they know that we're coming, that would be excellent."

The President responded, saying, "We'll have official papers drawn up by tomorrow, and we'll send official documentation to the field unit giving you red carpet treatment."

"That would be fine sir," replied Starr.

This came close to concluding the meeting except for a pretty decent snack provided by the White House chefs.

❧⚬⚬❧

The next few days were pretty busy for Starr and Matthew. They put together a portable diagnostic unit with an extended power supply. The readouts were clear, and the user interface was easy to operate.

"What do you think?" Matthew asked Starr.

"Pretty impressive for less than one week of work. Now for a field trial," replied Starr. "I expect that this should help out tremendously."

Halfway across the world, Colonel Rhodes opened a priority secure electronic mail message from the President. After looking at it, his eyes opened wide.

Colonel Rhodes called to his company clerk, "Mr. Hubble, get the senior staff in here immediately. No excuses from anyone."

"Yes sir," came the reply.

A few minutes later, a handful of people came in. There was Major Hunter, the head nurse, and Captains Stevens, Fisher, and Dixon, all surgeons. Once they were all seated, Colonel Rhodes spoke up.

"I just received a message from the President."

"You mean, THE President?" asked Major Hunter.

"You got it," replied the Colonel. "Within a few days we're going to get some VIPs here. These are no ordinary VIPs. This happens to be Dr. Matthew and Starr Carpenter. I'm guessing you people know who they are."

Dr. Dixon spoke up, "Yes, I just read an article in the *Richmond Medical Journal* from Dr. Carpenter and his work on diagnosing very rare forms of cancer earlier than anything known to medical science thus far."

"And isn't Starr the one that saved the First Lady and stopped the Harboni/Mern war?" interrupted Major Hunter.

"Same people," replied the Colonel. "I expect you people to provide them the utmost in cooperation. According to the

President and Secretary of Defense, anyone giving them the least amount of trouble can expect an immediate court martial. Do you all understand?"

They all shook their heads in the affirmative.

Dr. Stevens piped up with a wisecrack as usual, "I understand that Starr is single."

"Yes, but if she can stop a war single handedly, she wouldn't have much trouble dealing with you," replied the Major.

One more thing said the Colonel, "Starr will be bunking with Major Hunter, and Dr. Carpenter will be staying with you doctors. Understood?"

Again, they all nodded their heads in the affirmative.

Matthew and Starr said goodbyes to their family and then they transported to the Army post that was within a few miles of the hospital. There, they introduced themselves to the officer in charge, and he arranged for them to get a ride to the hospital.

As the vehicle approached the hospital, there appeared to be significant commotion in the compound. Matthew asked the driver what was going on.

"Looks like they just got a new batch of wounded, doctor," replied the driver. And with a sigh said, "welcome to the Middle East."

Matthew and Starr got out of the vehicle, and the driver unloaded their luggage and equipment.

Starr quickly ran over to the wounded to see what she could do. She hadn't seen wounded like this since the Harboni/Mern war. It was very bad. She quickly identified the order in which they should be taken care of when she eyed a soldier that she felt she should look at.

Major Hunter came over and blurted out, "Who are you and what are you doing here?"

Starr looked at her and said, "I'm Starr Carpenter. I was checking on the patients that needed the most attention."

This took Major Hunter by surprise, but then she said, "We'll deal with introductions later, but I don't think you need to deal with that one, he's already dead."

"Then that's exactly the one I'll start with," replied Starr.

With that she stood up and said "Starr power, activate." Immediately, there was a bright flash and she was transformed into Starr Gazer. She bent down and began talking to her on-board computer.

Major Hunter was stunned and just watched from a few feet away.

"Computer, analyze the patient, stop any more deterioration," declared Starr. "Can the patient be saved?"

The computer responded with, "patient has been dead longer than ten minutes. It will take 23 peta-watts to restore the patient to 97% capability."

"What functions will be compromised?" asked Starr.

"Three percent brain function will be lost."

"Can we limit it to past memory?"

"Affirmative."

"Proceed with the repair. How long will the repair take?"

"Six minutes twenty-three seconds with a one time power recharge."

Starr looked at Major Hunter and said, "Now we wait." After a few seconds, Starr continued, "Major, you're welcome to look after the other patients. I can take care of this one."

"I've never seen anything like this before. I'd like to stay if you don't mind."

"That's fine. Maybe you could at least check on some of the other patients to see which ones could use my attention next."

"Okay, I'll be back in a few minutes."

As the time approached, Major Hunter, the resident priest Father Nixon and Colonel Rhodes came over to see Starr and her patient.

The computer announced, "Repair complete. Bringing heartbeat, respiration and other vital signs to normal. Stimulating patient to consciousness."

The patient started breathing, and within fifteen seconds he moved his head and then opened his eyes. A few seconds later he started talking.

"Where am I?"

Starr looked at Major Hunter and spoke up, "Can you check him out while I go work on some of the other patients?"

"Yes, of course," she replied.

Matthew diagnosed most of the other new patients while Starr repaired the ones he prioritized. When the new patients were healed, Starr transformed back to her normal self and joined her father with the hospital staff.

"Those were quite some fancy maneuvers, Dr. and Miss Carpenter. How 'bout coming into my office where we can all talk?" asked the Colonel.

"Lead the way," said Matthew.

After they all assembled in Colonel Rhodes office, he opened the conversation. "Welcome to our hospital. It's not much, but we do meatball surgery. Just enough to patch them up and get them to a better hospital where more extensive surgery can be performed."

Matthew broke in and said, "The President has asked Starr and myself to build a unit that can assist you in a better diagnosis so that you can get to the root of the problem quicker, save more lives and get the patients as much functionality as possible. The first question that people have is why we can't just send some of my machines like I built for hospitals back home. The question is a matter of power. You simply don't have enough power in a front line hospital to rebuild people. The next question is why we couldn't just get Starr to go into every conflict and just take over. Well, she would probably kill off more people than would be done in a standard conflict. It would just all be on the same side of the conflict.

"So we've built a diagnostic unit, and we're here to do field trials and possibly leave it with you once you've been trained how to use it.

"We'd like to start first thing in the morning if you don't mind. Is there some place we can hook a laptop up to a projector so that a group of people could be trained in the principles of the unit before working on live people?"

Colonel Rhodes replied, "Yes, the mess hall is the best spot. We can start right after breakfast, say 9AM."

"That'll work," said Matthew.

"Good, 9 it is," said the Colonel. "Major, how about you taking Starr over to your tent and getting her settled before supper? Captain Dixon, could you take Dr. Carpenter to your tent?"

Both Major Hunter and Captain Dixon agreed. Starr followed Major Hunter to her quarters, and then Starr unpacked some of her belongings on the cot the Major assigned her. Starr looked at the Major who looked in her late 30's and decided to start up a conversation.

"Major?"

"Yes Miss Carpenter?"

"Are you always this formal?"

"Usually," replied Major Hunter.

"You're welcome to call me Starr," She said with a smile. "I deal with a lot of high ranking officials in the government and try to be informal when I can. I'm not that much of an ogre, am I?"

That brought a smile to the Major's face. "Okay Starr, and you can call me Maggie. That'll be something special just between you and me."

"How much do you know about my father and myself?" asked Starr.

"Only a few far-fetched tales actually. It wasn't till this afternoon when you healed all those people that I began to understand that the stories weren't just a bunch of bologna."

"I know that it's a little hard to believe, but we are real people with needs like anyone else. The only thing my father and I don't need is sleep. So Maggie, is there anything special that you'd like since you're so far away from home?"

Maggie thought for a minute and smiled saying, "I could use some nice hose, some decent chocolate, and some good hand cream. It really gets hot and dry here as you can well imagine."

Starr smiled and said, "I'll see what I can do. By the way, when was the last time any of you people had a decent meal beyond what the army provides?"

Maggie thought and said, "Now that's been a while too. At least six months I'd say."

"How many people do you have in this camp?" asked Starr.

"I think it was 85 at last count."

"I'll keep that in mind," replied Starr.

Starr thought for a second and asked, "Do you mind if I look at the men in recovery?"

"Sure we have a few minutes before supper."

The two walked down to the recovery area, and Starr went in with Maggie. There was a lot of commotion as the nurses were keeping a close eye on the patients for any signs of infection.

Starr noticed one man who couldn't have been much more than twenty years old. He was really dejected and Starr decided to ask Maggie what his situation was.

"Sad story," replied Maggie. "We had to amputate his leg. It was far too bad to save. He was a high school runner and hoped to run some in college after he got out of the service."

Starr felt really bad for him and decided to strike up a conversation with him.

"Hi. My name is Starr. What's yours?"

The soldier looked at her and sighed. "I'm Private Kaplan. They used to call me Lightning."

"Nice to meet you, Lightning. Is there anything special I can get for you?"

"Yeah, a new leg would be nice."

Starr was touched but she already knew what she had in mind to do. She just smiled and said, "You just rest and I'll be back a little later."

Starr pulled Maggie aside and said, "When we give our training tomorrow morning we're going to throw in something extra. We're giving Mr. Lightning a new leg."

"But how?" asked Maggie.

"My father did this once with his original machine. It's a matter of cloning but using a reverse image from the good leg. Something that will be very important will be for the brain to send the proper signals to the right muscles. That will take a little physical therapy. It should start as soon as the transformation is complete. Please keep that in mind." A shocked Maggie just responded with, "I certainly will. You people are really amazing."

"Just helping out where we can."

As it was time for supper, Starr and Maggie joined Matthew and the camp senior staff at the mess hall.

"Hey dad," said Starr. "There's a soldier with a leg that had to be amputated. I was thinking of cloning him a new one. He used to be a runner and was really depressed. I was going to wait till tomorrow but can we possibly do it after supper?"

Matthew smiled at Starr and said, "That's my girl, always thinking of others."

Dr. Dixon looked pretty surprised and spoke up, "That's amazing. I'd like to be present when you do that. He was my patient, and I'd like to see him fully recover. I was really feeling for him when we had to take the leg off."

Matthew nodded and said, "It's pretty cool to watch. We'll need all the bandages taken off so nothing is in the way."

After supper, Matthew, Starr, and the staff all headed to post-op where there were about a dozen soldiers in recovery. Matthew looked at the charts for each of them, the last one being Private Kaplan. All the soldiers except Kaplan had wounds that had a chance of full recovery without intervention from Starr. Remember that Starr's accelerated healing and rebuilding processes were based on the *Healing Machine* that her father had built and were really meant for terminally ill patients or ones that did not have much hope for a meaningful life without intervention. In Private Kaplan's case, he was so young and had such high hopes of continuing his ability to run, the Carpenters decided that it was in the best interest of Private Kaplan to provide him with a new leg that was fully functional and not any sort of artificial one that most hospitals would provide.

When Matthew and Starr got to Private Kaplan, a whole horde of spectators came with them including all the doctors on staff, Maggie, and Autumn an attending nurse.

Matthew looked at Maggie and Autumn and then at Private Kaplan and then spoke to the Private, "Hello. My name is Dr. Carpenter. I understand that you were a pretty good runner."

Private Kaplan seemed pretty bitter but said, "Yes, once."

When Matthew realized how depressed and angry the patient was, he said, "Well, let's see if we can help get you back on your feet. Notice I said feet and not foot."

In a very suspicious tone the private responded with, "What do you mean, doc?"

With a smile, Starr said, "We're going to give you a new leg. Just stay calm, and we'll get you back together and able to run marathons in no time. The entire procedure should not take more than half an hour. After that, a little physical therapy, and you should be walking pretty soon."

Matthew looked at Maggie and Autumn. "Could you please uncover the leg bandages and remove any sheets? We'll take it from there."

Maggie and Autumn began removing bandages and blood started oozing out. As Starr noticed what could happen with a possible hemorrhage, she decided to transform.

"Starr power, activate," she said.

Once the flash from the bright light died down, she said "Computer, analyze patient. Stop any more blood loss."

"Acknowledged," came the voice over the speaker in her suit.

At once, the oozing slowed to a halt and Maggie and Autumn could remove the rest of the bandages without there being any hemorrhaging.

"Good thinking, daughter," Matthew said as he smiled at Starr.

"Thought it would be a good idea," she replied.

"Computer, analyze the right leg, perform a reverse image and clone it to build his left leg. Attempt to give each of the nerves in the new leg their own identity so that they will not revert to right leg properties. How long will the process take?"

"Acknowledged," replied the computer. "Rebuilding will take 4 minutes 23 seconds."

Within seconds, the portion of the left leg on the upper thigh where the amputation took place began to change. The bone began to grow and when the entire femur was complete, the knee began to form. Once the knee formed, the tibia and fibula began to form. Once these were complete, the ankle tarsus, metatarsal, and the various phalanx formed.

"This is incredible," Maggie said.

The entire staff agreed, and a number of other patients came over to see as well.

Once all the bones were in place, the various ligaments and tendons formed, then the muscles and nerves, and finally the skin and hair.

Matthew spoke to the crowd and said, "Note that the left leg is now identical to the right in all features. They're just reverse images of each other."

The computer voice broke in with, "Repair complete. Allowing normal nerve and blood flow processes to proceed and function on their own. Performing final analysis to verify integrity of the repair."

Five seconds later, the computer voice continued with, "Analysis complete. Patient is in satisfactory condition."

Starr breathed a sigh of relief and transformed back to her normal self.

Matthew looked at Private Kaplan and said. "Okay, the rest is up to you and the physical therapists here. It's possible that your left leg won't react perfectly to your commands quite yet. It may still think it's a right leg. Let's give it a try. I want you to move your right big toe."

Private Kaplan wiggled his right toe but his left big toe also began to wiggle.

Matthew looked at Private Kaplan and said, "Now I want you to concentrate really hard on your left big toe and try to move it."

At first it didn't move at all, and everyone could see Private Kaplan concentrate hard. Then it started to move a little. The more he concentrated, the more it moved, and within a couple of minutes he could wiggle it reasonably well.

Matthew looked at Nurse Autumn, "Could you please work with Private Kaplan on some physical therapy? He should be able to be walking on his own within a day or so. Remember in the early stages, it's a matter of controlling the proper muscles. In addition, the nerves need to react as well. So, make sure that you provide lots of touch on the legs. First one leg, then the other. Don't have him get up until you can tickle the bottom of each foot independently and get a proper reaction from each foot. That would be a good sign he wouldn't fall from getting sensations from the wrong foot."

"Understood", replied the nurse.

Starr and Maggie decided to retire for the evening, or at least that's what Starr led Maggie to believe. When they arrived at their quarters, Maggie looked on her bed and was in complete shock. There were the most beautiful pairs of pantyhose she'd ever seen, a dozen boxes of exquisite chocolates, and some bottles of goat milk hand lotion.

Maggie looked at Starr and then at the gifts and started crying. "Nobody's done anything like this for me before. They think I'm just always formal and no fun."

Maggie gave Starr a big hug and said, "Thank you."

Starr was very touched and said, "You seemed like you could use a friend. I thought I'd oblige. Think about it like an early Christmas present."

Maggie smiled and said, "You have no idea how much this means to me."

Starr said, "You enjoy your treasure, and then get some sleep. I'll be up talking to my father for a while."

Starr left Maggie to enjoy her new toys and went off to find her father. She found him at the quarters where the other staff doctors were. As she walked in, her father smiled. "So, number one," he said. "What have you been up to in the last hour?"

Starr looked at him and with a smile said, "Just making people happy as usual."

Matthew shook his head and was about to say something when they heard a noise from outside.

"What's that?" asked Dr. Dixon. "It sounds like a plane, but it is awful close."

The next thing they heard was a big explosion. A split second later the lights went out.

Starr and Matthew went outside as the plane turned for another pass. Starr immediately transformed and took the plane out of the sky with a single shot though it was still about a half mile away. Everyone then went over to the generator to see what the problem was.

"Looks like it wasn't the generator itself but just one of the cables between the generator and the transformer," one of the technicians said.

"How long to fix?" asked Colonel Rhodes.

"We don't have the cable in stock, Colonel. It'll be tomorrow before we can get a new one."

Starr looked at the damage and realized that it was the cable from only one of the phases that was broken. It looked like the cable took a shrapnel hit causing the break in the cable. It was about two feet short of where it should be.

"That's only one phase that's out, isn't it?" she asked.

"That's right, miss. But that's the one that has all the lights. The other two phases are used for the medical equipment. It would take time to rewire the lights to another phase."

Starr looked around for anything she could use to patch the cable but didn't find anything useful. She then asked the technician, "Is there anything around here that could be used to repair the cable until it could be replaced?"

"We have some cable about the right size but we'd have to take the entire generator off-line to make the repair and it would take several hours," he replied.

"Could you go get a few feet of the cable and come back quickly?" she asked.

"Sure thing," he said.

As he ran off to get the cable, Matthew looked at Starr and smiled. A minute later, the technician brought the cable and handed it to Starr.

Starr looked at the cable in her hand and then at the frazzled segments that were both ends of the now dangling pieces of the missing phase. She used her on-board laser at 1% power to clean off both ends of the piece of cable in her hand. She then cleaned the pieces of the lines that were connected to both the transformer and the generator. Once the pieces were ready, she increased power to 2% and welded the cable in place, first at the generator end and then at the transformer end. Once the cable to the transformer began touching the cable to the generator, the lights began to flicker. Once the welding was finished, the lights came back on bright.

Starr looked at the technician and asked, "Do you have anything I could use for insulation?"

"I was thinking about that," he replied. "Here's some cable insulation we had from other wire we jury rigged."

"Perfect," she said.

With that she wrapped the insulation around the wire and with 0.1% laser power managed to seal it off. With a sigh of relief, she transformed back to her regular clothes.

Maggie came up to her and gave her a hug. When Maggie let go, and they could look each other in the eyes, Starr just winked at her.

The training the next day went without a hitch, and the staff learned how to use the new equipment rather quickly. As everything was going well for a change, Matthew and Starr came up with a plan to treat the entire staff including any troops in recovery. They told the mess crew to take the afternoon off so that they didn't have to do anything with the evening meal. They had talked with the President, who arranged to have a set of caterers ready for transport. Starr performed the transport of all the caterers and food to the mess tent from many thousands of miles away, and once the meal was ready, she asked the colonel permission to talk over the loud speaker. The colonel spoke first to get the attention of everyone.

"Attention everyone," he said. "Starr would like to have a word with all of you."

After handing the microphone over to her, she began. "Hello everyone. You've all been a great bunch while we've been here and we'd like to extend our thanks by providing a meal for you this afternoon. The menu consists of the following: a full salad bar with everything from fresh tender spinach to exotic mushrooms and olives; your choice of fresh hot white, cracked wheat, and molasses rolls with fresh butter, strawberry preserves and apple butter; main courses of lobster, crab, shrimp, scallops, and clams in various forms such as fried, baked and spiced, additional main courses of frog legs, leg of lamb, Swiss steak, chicken Kiev, and schnitzel, side dishes of German red cabbage, corn pudding, scalloped potatoes, candied sweet potatoes, green bean casserole, and stewed tomatoes, desserts of carrot cake, German chocolate cake, Black Forest cake, cherry pie, wineberry pie, French silk pie, homemade ice cream flavors of coconut, strawberry, and chocolate, gourmet coffees in various flavors, additional drinks of iced tea, fresh squeezed lemonade, lime Rickeys, and apple cider and some fresh fruit such as pineapple, cherries, grapes, figs, and kiwi. There should easily be enough for everyone, so you don't have to trample down anyone to get there. We don't need any more casualties than we already have. We'll see you there after a while. Think about it like an early Christmas dinner. Bon appetit."

The colonel just stared at Starr and Matthew with his mouth open for a second until Matthew snapped him out of it by snapping his fingers. Then Matthew motioned for the colonel to just follow them to the mess tent.

As they moved in the direction of the mess tent, the lines were quite long, but since there were only about 100 people it wasn't going to be nearly as long as it seemed at the time. Within 30 minutes, everyone had been served and was happily eating and drinking to their hearts' content. The joking and laughing could be heard all the way on the other side of the compound.

Starr smiled at her father and said, "I think this was a pretty good hit and about what they really needed."

"So you think it's just what the doctor ordered?" he asked with a smile and a snicker.

"Ha Ha, dad," she replied.

After the meal was over, the group bedded down for the night (all except Matthew and Starr of course) and though full, still slept with smiles of contentment on their faces.

❦

The next morning the camp awoke to the sound of helicopter transports. These were the type that were used to transport the wounded to the hospital. As everyone prepared to deal with the patients, Starr and Matthew thought this would be an excellent time to have the staff use the portable analyzer in a live situation.

Dr. Dixon was the first doctor to get to a patient but was very taken aback by what he saw. The patient's eyes were moving in violent circles, and the patient's hands and legs were shaking. He attempted to use the analyzer on the patient but didn't understand what the readings were telling him. Matthew and Starr were about 20 feet away and noticed the reactions of both Dr. Dixon and the patient. Starr and Matthew looked at each other and decided to go investigate.

"What's the problem?" Matthew asked Dr. Dixon.

"I don't understand what's going on. I've never seen reactions like this in any of our patients before."

As he said this, the other patients being brought over to the diagnostic area were exhibiting similar symptoms.

Matthew took over the handling of the analyzer and began a diagnosis. What he saw on the monitor frightened him, and he showed the results to Starr. She knew what she had to do next and transformed.

She bent down and placed her hands on the patient. "Computer?" she said. "Analyze the patient."

Five seconds later the computer responded. "Patient has been exposed to a combination of both biological and chemical agents. The responses being exhibited by the patient are caused by the agents attacking the nervous system."

"Can we clean the patient's entire system?"

"Affirmative. But it is recommended that his clothes be removed and destroyed to eliminate any possibility of recontamination."

The closest doctors and nurses began removing the soldier's clothing and realized that they themselves may be contaminated.

"Computer, can you decontaminate all of us at the same time?"

"Yes, but those that are already affected internally will need to be decontaminated individually."

"Proceed with the general decontamination."

"Understood," responded the computer.

With that Starr's entire suit glowed, and there was a bright light that went out to all the staff and patients. Within 15 seconds the glow began to dissipate.

"General decontamination complete," spoke the computer over Starr's intercom.

"Okay," said Starr. "Let's start with an internal decontamination of the first patient."

The computer complied. Once the first patient was conscious, Starr worked on the other dozen that were also affected in this batch of patients.

In the meantime, Matthew and the colonel began asking the soldiers what happened.

The leader of the squad, Sergeant Nicholas, spoke for the group. "We were climbing over a rise and began taking on fire. Suddenly, an explosion happened about 100 yards in the air, and we felt this dust cover us. Within a minute we began to feel very sick and fell to the ground. We couldn't control our muscles at all. The next thing we knew we were here at your hospital."

"Do you have any idea how you got here?" asked the colonel.

"Not a clue."

"We'll need to decontaminate the medics and choppers," noted the colonel. "Major Hunter, get a call out to all the other hospitals to be on the lookout for people with these symptoms, and get them to us. Anyone handling those people should also be brought over."

"Yes, Colonel," Maggie replied before running off to comply with the order.

"Now what?" asked the colonel looking at Matthew and Starr.

Starr looked at her father and said, "I think we need to talk to the President. I'm thinking about stopping the bloodshed before any more soldiers come back like these men did." With that she called the President on her internal communications. Once he picked up, she began the conversation.

"Mr. President, we have a situation here. The enemy has begun using biological and chemical weapons. I believe it's time we end the war before too many people are killed and maimed for life. I'd like permission to proceed."

"I understand, Starr. By the authority invested in me as Commander in Chief, I hereby authorize you to proceed and attempt to stop the bloodshed using whatever force is necessary."

Starr responded with, "Thank you, sir. I'll get Colonel Rhodes to get in touch with all the commanders in the field to pull back so there will be few casualties from our side. Over and out."

With that, Starr hung up and looked at the Colonel. "I'm guessing you heard the conversation. Please get in touch with as many commanders as possible to get the troops out of harm's way. I'll take care of the rest."

"I'll get right on it, Starr," replied the colonel.

With that out of the way, she looked at her father and asked, "Any last words before I tackle the enemy, dad?"

Matthew thought carefully and said, "Not really. You've done this sort of thing before. I would just recommend that you take prisoner as many of the high officials as possible."

"I agree," she replied. She smiled and then said, "I love you, dad. See you in a couple of hours."

With that, Starr vanished in a flash of light.

Starr reappeared where she thought the highest chances of the enemy would be and set all sensors to maximum. One by one she picked out the enemy strongholds and missile launchers and obliterated them. Since she really wasn't sure where the heads of state were, she decided to talk to General Taggart.

"General, this is Starr Gazer. I've eliminated all of the enemy and have stopped any additional casualties from the biological and chemical weapons. I need to know an approximate location of any of the leaders of the rebellion."

"Good work, Starr. That will help us immensely. If we knew the location of the leaders, we'd have taken them out by now. That's the problem with terrorists and subversives. You don't know where they are. Sorry, we can't help you."

With a sigh she said, "Okay, general. I'll see what I can find out on my own."

"I figured out where all the rest were, I guess I can figure out where these guys are as well," Starr thought to herself.

Starr thought for a minute and decided to time warp to the location of one of the major missile launchers she had obliterated. Once there, she time-warped backwards like you would play a DVD backwards at high speed. At one point in time, she noticed the leader of the launcher group talking on his radio. She traced the call to a higher ranking leader. After doing several more traces of other leaders, she finally hit the jackpot. This new leader was not killed by her in any of her other raids. She took note of his location and who he was and then performed a few other traces from that particular leader. Within a short time she had the names and locations of a dozen high ranking officials. By that point she decided to call General Taggart.

"General, this is Starr again."

"Yes, Starr. What can I do for you?"

"I have the locations of a dozen high ranking officials. I will capture them one by one and transport them to your location. Please get ready to arrest and interrogate them."

"Excellent work. We'll be prepared. Thanks."

Starr then got to work and within an hour had found, captured, and transported the highest ranking officials in the enemy organization to the location of General Taggart where they were immediately arrested.

Once Starr had finished, she transported back to the hospital where the staff was waiting patiently with additional contaminated soldiers. Once she decontaminated them, she breathed a sigh of relief and finally transformed back to her normal self.

Maggie was there and immediately gave her a hug. "You're a very special young lady, Starr, and by the way, Merry Christmas." she said with a loving smile.

Starr looked at her, winked and said, "And a very Merry Christmas to you too, Maggie. And... you're not so bad yourself."

They both started laughing as Matthew came over to them. "I know there's trouble brewing every time two girls get together and laugh."

Starr and Maggie just looked at each other and giggled all the more.

Chapter 8

Starr of the West

"Okay, Agent Thompson," said Starr. "You can tell the President that the problem in Arizona has been taken care of. As soon as I transform and get back in my suit, I'll transport back home. I'm ready to come home for Christmas."

"Understood, Starr. Good work as usual."

Starr could hear the rumble of thunder in the distance. "Looks like there's a storm that's about to break, so I should get back as soon as I can," Starr responded.

"See you soon, Starr. Goodbye," the agent replied.

Starr was glad this case was over. She couldn't wait to get back home. It had been three days of intense work, and she thought she really needed a break. With a big sigh she said, "Starr power, activate."

As soon as she started to transform, a lightning bolt hit her suit, and she blacked out.

"Well, Marshall," said Deputy Jonathan Wheeler. "How long do you think it'll be before we catch up with the Dalton gang?"

The deputy was not as quick on the draw as the Marshall and not quite as astute, but he was very loyal and honest. He and the Marshall had been trailing the 6 person gang for 2 days and expected that they were pretty close. The horses could use a little rest so they stopped by a stream to give them about 10 minutes rest before starting again.

Marshall Frank Fulton was very quick on the draw and as honest as they come. He was in his 40's and an excellent horseman and cattleman. He was well respected in Tucson and always did the right thing.

The Marshall got off his horse and inspected the hoof prints from the horses they were following.

"I'd say they're only a few hours ahead of us," he replied. "If we keep going, we should be able to catch up to them. Looks like they're not traveling too fast. My guess is that one of them is hurt and it's slowing them down."

After a few minutes they got back on their horses and were about to ride away when a flash of light blinded them, and it was all the two men could do to control their horses.

"What the heck was that Marshall?" asked the deputy.

The Marshall was a rather observant man and quickly scanned the area for anything unusual. About 100 feet away was something on the ground that the Marshall couldn't quite make out.

"I think I see something over there on the ground about 100 feet off. You see it?" replied the Marshall.

Jonathan looked to where Frank pointed and nodded. They both headed their horses in that direction and got there in a matter of seconds. What they saw was like nothing they had seen before. It sort of looked like a person but dressed up like no person they could have identified.

"Looks like it's hurt Jonathan. Let's see what we can do."

They dismounted and went over to the thing and turned it over. As they did so, it began to stir and they stepped back.

"Should we pull out our guns?" asked Jonathan.

"No I don't think so," replied Frank. "Whatever it is it won't likely hurt us. If anything it needs our help."

After another minute the thing could be heard saying, "Computer, are you functional?"

"Affirmative," came the answer over the intercom.

"Good. Run a complete set of diagnostics. Let me know what's not working."

Starr looked up and realized she wasn't alone. She got up and looked around.

"Where am I?" she asked the people before her.

"You're about 100 miles outside Tucson," replied the Marshall. "Now how 'bout if I ask you who you are?"

"I'm Starr Carpenter, Code name Starr Gazer and I'm with the US Secret Service. Now exactly who are you?"

"I'm Marshall Frank Fulton and this is Deputy Jonathan Wheeler. I don't know anything about any US Secret Service."

Starr thought for a minute and asked the computer for a damage report.

"Invisibility mode is non-functional as well as all of the time circuits."

"Can they be repaired?" she asked.

"The solar prisms were damaged, and thus invisibility mode cannot be repaired in this location. The time circuits have been heavily damaged but repair can take place in about 43 hours 23 minutes."

"That'll have to do. Can you repair the suit without me being in it?"

"Affirmative"

"Go for it," replied Starr.

Starr realized that the two men were still standing there and didn't quite know what to think.

"Excuse me while I transform back to my normal clothes," said Starr. "Starr power deactivate."

With that, another blinding light appeared and after it dissipated, Starr was there in a t-shirt and jeans with a US Secret Service ball cap on.

"Well, it's a girl," said Jonathan. "She can't be much more than 17."

"I can see that," answered the Marshall. He looked at Starr and said, "Now just what are you doing out here in the middle of nowhere?"

"Before I answer that, what year is this?"

"I'm guessing you must have had quite a bump on the head for you not to know what year this is. It's 1850, miss."

Starr realized this would be an interesting two days.

"Oh boy. Looks like I'm stuck here for two days while my suit is getting repaired. Okay, Marshall. I probably owe you an explanation, so you may want to sit down for a while."

"We don't have lots of time, miss. We're after a gang of outlaws. They held up a bank in Tucson, and we've been tracking them for a couple of days now."

"I'll help you catch them in a little while. You should listen to me first."

The Marshall smiled and said, "You're going to help us catch them? This is a job for the law, miss. I don't exactly think you're the type to be helping us. Besides, we're probably only a few hours ride behind them, I should be after them now."

"Marshall, I'm sure that girls in your time period are not the type to go hunting for outlaws. But where I come from, it's a little different."

The Marshall looked at her a little funny and said, "What do you mean by *your time period*?"

Starr smiled and said, "I'm from the 21st century. I got struck by lightning and was transported to this time."

She pulled out her badge identification from her hip pocket and showed it to the Marshall. His eyes grew wide and he shook his head.

"You mean that you're from the future?"

"That's right. I'm temporarily caught in the past, your past, and I've got to wait for my suit, that is, my transportation back to the future to be repaired before I go back."

The Marshall just scratched his head and said, "Since we're in the middle of nowhere, we've got to figure out what to do with you."

"Well, how about if I go catch those crooks for you, and you can just catch up when you get there? Remember Marshall, I work for the law as well."

"Maybe, but not in this time."

"I gave an oath to uphold the law regardless of the circumstances. I expect you did something similar."

The Marshall smiled and said, "You win. So what are you going to do?"

"Just watch," she said. "Starr power activate."

After another flash of light that they were now getting used to, she appeared in her suit again and started speaking to her computer.

"Computer, can I use the suit for non-damaged functions while you are repairing it?"

"Affirmative."

"Great. Arm weapon systems to heavy stun. Set force field on."

With that, Starr took the controls using her telepathic interface and began leaving the ground gaining altitude to about 100 yards. The men just stared in disbelief. She then found the tracks the horses of the gang members had left and followed them at about half the speed of sound. It didn't take very long for her to catch up to them, and she landed about a hundred feet in front of them. The horses were scared and several of the men were thrown to the ground. All of them began firing on Starr and luckily the force field held up. With a few quick shots from her heavy stun weapons, they were out cold in no time. She then rounded up the horses, tied up the men and loaded them on their horses. Within a few minutes they were on their way back to meet the Marshall and deputy. About an hour and a half later, the two parties met.

"Well I wouldn't have believed it if I hadn't seen it with my own eyes," exclaimed Jonathan.

"I have to admit, I'm the same way," said Frank.

Starr rode over on one of the horses and met the law men. She had already transformed back to her regular clothes and had just led the prisoners along.

"Here are your prisoners, Marshall," Starr said with a smile.

Marshall Fulton shook his head and smiled.

"You can be on my team anytime, Starr. Now we just have to get back to Tucson. It'll be dark in a few hours so we won't be making much headway tonight."

"I think I can manage a little better than that Marshall," Starr replied. "I think I can transport everyone at the same time and get you back there in a flash. I'll meet you there a couple of minutes later. You game for trying a teleport?"

The Marshall looked at Starr with a very doubting gaze.

"Aw come on, Marshall. You'll be fine," Starr said as she chuckled.

Frank nodded and said, "What do we do?"

"Just get everyone, including the horses as close together as you can. I'll do the rest."

The next thing that Frank, Jonathan, and the prisoners knew, they were in Tucson in front of the jail.

"That's the wildest thing I've ever experienced," said Jonathan.

"It worked, and I actually feel fine," answered Frank.

The horses seemed a little spooked, but they calmed down quickly. Once the prisoners were locked up, Starr walked into the Sheriff's office and met Frank.

"Hello, Marshall. I see you have everything under control."

"Yes, thanks to your help we've got the entire Dalton gang behind bars." The Marshall looked at Starr and said, "What are you going to do now?"

"I'm not exactly sure. I've got about two days to kill. Got any suggestions?"

Frank looked at her and said, "You probably deserve a reward for capturing the gang, but I'm not sure you can use it where you're going."

Just then the door opened and Katie walked in. Katie was the saloon owner and a good friend of Marshall Fulton's.

"Hello, Frank," said Katie. "I hear you caught the Daltons. Is everyone okay?"

Katie was in her 30's and a very pretty lady. Starr had never seen women's clothes from that time period up close. This was a real history lesson for her. Katie looked at Starr with a rather odd sort of look considering the clothes that Starr was wearing.

"Yes, everyone's fine thanks to my friend, Starr, here," spoke the Marshall. "By the way, this is Starr Carpenter. She'll be our guest in Tucson for a couple of days. Could she get a room at your place? I'll pick up the tab. If there's anything she needs, get it for her."

"Sure Frank, no trouble at all."

"Starr, go along with Katie. She'll take good care of you. How 'bout if I see you for supper at about 5:30?" asked Frank.

"That's fine, Marshall. I'll be glad to join you." Starr looked at her digital watch and set the alarm for 5:15. That made everyone in the office just stare in amazement at what that thing on Starr's arm really was.

"Jonathan, why don't you show Starr around town and then bring her over to Katie's in a little while?"

"Sure thing, Marshall," he replied.

Jonathan and Starr left the office, and Katie just looked bewildered.

"Starr is with the US Secret Service," said Frank.

"The what?" asked Katie.

"Starr is from the future. She got caught in some sort of time problem and is stuck here for a few days."

"You don't actually believe that do you?" asked Katie.

"I believe every word of it. If you'd have seen what I did and had your cells moved two days journey in a matter of seconds and seen her catch the entire Dalton gang single-handedly, you'd believe it too. What I need from you is to help her get accustomed to the area and keep her out of trouble."

"I'll see what I can do," she replied.

Katie left and Frank just shook his head. "I still don't believe it," he said laughingly to himself.

Jonathan showed Starr around town and then brought her over to the saloon where Katie had rooms upstairs.

Starr looked around at the saloon and smiled. "I've never been to a real saloon before Miss Katie."

"I'm sure you haven't. You don't look much more than 17."

Starr was quite amused as Katie brought her up to her room. There wasn't much in the way of furniture. There was a bed, a table with a wash basin on it, a towel, a couple of chairs and a place to put clothes.

"Is there a library in Tucson?" asked Starr.

"There's a small one a couple of streets over," replied Katie.

"I've got another hour and a half before I meet Marshall Fulton for supper so I thought I'd check out some of the books from this time period."

Katie just looked at Starr and asked, "You really aren't from around here are you?"

"No ma'am," she replied.

Katie left Starr in her room, and Starr decided to take a walk around town. She went by the mercantile, the barber shop, the bank, the livery stable, the blacksmith, and eventually over to the library. When she got there she walked in and realized that it wasn't that big. The entire library wasn't more than 12 feet by 25 feet. Even so, there were some interesting books there. Obviously there was nothing from after 1850. She did find some interesting works from Benjamin Franklin that she hadn't seen before. This kept her amused till her watch beeped for supper. She got up and walked outside and began retracing her steps back to the saloon where supper was to be.

When she got within sight of it, she heard a shot and then another one. Deputy Wheeler stumbled outside the saloon and fell on the ground as a man followed him outside, gun in hand. The next thing Starr saw was the man getting on a horse and riding out of town. Marshall Fulton rushed over and examined Jonathan just as Starr arrived.

"He's dead," said the Marshall.

Doc Gilbert ran over and examined Jonathan.

"There's nothing I can do for him, Frank," said the doctor.

The Marshall looked at Starr with an inquisitive look and asked, "Is there anything you can do?"

Starr nodded and said, "I'll take care of it, sir."

With that response she transformed and nearly frightened everyone in the area except Frank. She then bent down and placed her hands on Jonathan's chest. A red glow came from her hands as the computer analyzed the patient and repaired him. When Starr had finished the repair, Jonathan regained consciousness and looked at Starr.

"I should have known it would be you that would help me out," Jonathan said.

Frank looked at Starr and said, "Thanks."

Starr just nodded. "Do you mind if I go get the guy who did this? I'll be back in a couple of minutes. Keep supper hot for me."

"Go right ahead, Starr," he replied with a smile.

With that, Starr ascended a few hundred feet and headed after the outlaw. Some people in the street screamed while others just stared. It didn't take more than a couple of minutes for Starr to come back with the man in tow.

"What took you so long?" chuckled Jonathan.

"I didn't think there was any rush," replied Starr.

The outlaw looked at Jonathan and said, "I thought I killed you."

"You did," replied Jonathan. "You're looking at a ghost."

Jonathan put his hands on his head and said "Boo!"

The man reeled back in surprise and then with a quick jerk, Marshall Fulton dragged him off to jail.

Starr looked at Jonathan, Katie, and Doc and said, "Now how 'bout some supper?"

Jonathan looked at Starr and said, "Don't you think you should change first?"

"Oops," she replied. And with that Starr transformed back into her normal clothes.

This made everyone in attendance except Jonathan very surprised and a little frightened. Once they got over the shock, Jonathan took Starr by the arm and they strolled over to the saloon, which wasn't particularly far away as Jonathan had died right outside of it. Frank met them there a few minutes later, and Starr asked what everyone would recommend to eat.

"I think the beef stew is pretty good," answered doc.

"I'd go for the chicken pot pie," replied Jonathan.

"I'm a steak man myself," said Frank.

Starr thought for a minute and said, "I'll be here for a couple of days so I'll get to try more than one thing. I think I'll try the beef stew. I'd like to see the difference 150 odd years makes in recipes and ingredients."

"One beef stew coming up," said Katie. "I know what you other boys want."

"Got any preferences on drinks?" asked Katie.

"What have you got in soft drinks?"

"We've got a good ginger ale and some excellent root beer."

"I'll try the ginger ale today and the root beer tomorrow," said Starr.

Starr looked at Jonathan with a smile and winked. "You should be fine. Your injuries were pretty minor."

Doc looked at Starr and said, "Minor! He had been shot twice and killed. I wouldn't exactly call that minor."

Starr looked at him and replied, "It's all relative, sir. Major injuries are ones that take more than one petawatt to repair. As a rule those injuries relate to some amount of brain damage. The more the damage, the more complex they are and the higher power to repair. Even something as complex as a shot through the lungs or heart is pretty easy."

Doc just looked at her in amazement. "That's incredible," was all he could say.

Within a few minutes the food came and Starr caught a whiff of the stew. "This smells really good."

It tasted even better and Starr asked for the recipe. Unlike the additives that people use in the 21st century, everything in 1850 was natural. A little of this spice or that can produce an excellent flavor. Starr looked at the actual ingredients and realized that they didn't use refined sugar and their vegetables were not the hybrid types we use today. Starr took careful notes and stuck them in her pocket.

There were no more surprises that evening and Starr went back to her room for the night. She had checked a couple of books out of the library so it gave her something to do since she couldn't sleep anyway.

The next morning Starr went over to the saloon for breakfast and had some pancakes and sausage. She asked Katie what they put in the sausage since she hadn't tasted these spices before.

"I don't know," she said. "Nothing particularly unusual. We use these chili peppers, some sage, coriander, pepper, and some salt."

Starr looked at the ingredients and took some careful notes on the exact types.

After breakfast she went down to see Marshall Fulton at the jail. "Good morning, sir," she said. "Anything new?"

"Hello, Starr," he replied with a smile. "Not really. The prisoners will be tried today. I did get word from the local fort that there could be trouble with some of the Indians."

"What sort of trouble?" asked Starr.

The Marshall looked pretty grim. "Normally there isn't much problem, but they've been pretty upset that the cattle ranchers are infringing on their hunting grounds, and the ranchers don't want the Indians around."

Starr looked pretty downcast and decided to discuss how history went with the Indians, ranchers, and the government. "It wasn't a part of history that was something to be proud of," she said. "There's nothing I should be doing about it since I don't really want to interfere in history any more than I already have. I'm actually concerned that I may have interfered too much as it is."

The Marshall looked at her very seriously and said, "A lot of people may die if something isn't done."

"That's right, but if I do something, a lot of history as I know it may change forever." She thought for a minute and then said, "Oh, I wish dad were here."

She decided to leave the office and go back to her room to pray. It seems like the incidents that had already taken place were not a problem with history since the Marshall was to take the Dalton gang anyway and it was going to take them 2 days to return to Tucson. Jonathan would not have died since he was to be with the Marshall at that time on his way back to Tucson. Thus, this problem with the Indian encounter would be the first time that anyone else would be heavily involved to the point where history may change.

Starr decided to get back in her suit and check any historical records about the encounter that was going to happen. She found nothing except a small note about some natural events that occasionally would stop some Indian uprisings. This gave Starr an idea. If she could make it appear like there was a supernatural event that happened, then maybe she could get both sides to go home without a fight. She decided to go by the Marshall's office and tell him of her idea.

"I think the best course of action would be for me to cause some problem to happen like a simulated earthquake as the two parties are about to meet. I could actually create a small divide in the earth and have it so the parties cannot meet each other."

"That would stop them for a time but it wouldn't stop them for long," replied the Marshall.

"True," Starr replied. "History will play out regardless of what I do."

Starr thought for another minute and said, "I could always appear before the tribe and have them think I'm one of their gods. No, that wouldn't work since that would be counter-productive to the true Gospel. Ah, but I could appear as one sent from God Himself."

Starr thought about it more, and she got a feeling that might be the right answer.

"What about the ranchers and soldiers?" asked the Marshall.

"That's where I'll need your help," she replied. "You need to talk to them to stay away from the Indian hunting areas, and the Indians will leave them alone."

"That won't work," indicated the Marshall, shaking his head. "These are stubborn ranchers. They think that they can roam anywhere they like. They can't even keep off each other's land, never mind trying to work well with the Indians."

"Then maybe I'll have to convince them to stay away from certain areas," replied Starr. "I may have to resort to force."

"I thought you weren't going to do that," he said with a rather stern look.

"I'll have to think it over and decide as I go along," she said. "I just won't have any more people getting killed than I have to. Can you arrest anyone that attempts to kill the Indians?"

"I can try," replied the Marshall. "But I don't know if I'd get any support. There are plenty of people that just want a place to live in peace, and then there are those that think the Indians aren't even people. Some of the settlers' relatives were killed by the Indians, so they may not be too receptive to being kind."

"It's always hard to point fingers for how an argument started," Starr declared. "Sometimes it's easier to just squelch it by force, though people are a very hard bunch to change. I'm going to start with visiting the Indians and see where that leads me."

"Fair enough," replied the Marshall.

Starr went outside and transformed. She then plotted a course to the Indian village 20 miles to the north east that was likely to cause the most problem. She was within 3 miles when she caught sight of it, and it began to worry her. There were thousands of Indians that appeared like they were getting prepared for war. Starr decided to make a dramatic entrance in order to make the point, and she hoped her built-in translator knew whatever language these Indians spoke.

She decided to make a bunch of noise as she came out of the sky and approach what appeared to be the center of the camp. The Indians saw her and were afraid, exactly the reaction she was hoping for. She landed and approached what appeared to be the main chief. Some of the braves drew their bows and fired at her but it had no affect against the force field. This caused them to be even more afraid.

"O great chief," Starr began. "What you are about to do is a mistake. You must not go on the war path. Many braves will die."

The chief looked at her and asked, "Who are you? Are you the great spirit?"

"No I am not, but I do come from Him. He does not want people killed, neither from your tribes nor from the white man's."

"How do I know that you are from the great spirit?" asked the chief. "It has not rained in many moons. The animals have to go far for water and go into the white man's lands. Can you make it rain, one who comes from the great spirit?"

"If I make it rain, will you not go on the war path?" asked Starr.

"We will not go," replied the chief.

Starr took flight and went straight up for several thousand feet while all the Indians looked up at her. She asked her computer the best way to get it to rain. It didn't appear like there were many clouds, so she'd have to try the hard way. A highly charged electric field covering about 500 square miles with just the right electric current might be enough to cause a storm. As she went about setting up the field, she began to feel the increase in the humidity level, and with just a little more current applied, she could feel a thunderstorm about to break. The lightning began, the thunder could be heard, and the water began to fall. She continued the current until the storm could maintain itself. It was a torrential downpour by the time she returned to the chief.

"O great chief," Starr began. "The rains have come. You must not go on the war path."

"We will not go," replied the chief.

"You are a brave man," Starr said. "I will now visit the white man and convince him to leave your people alone."

The chief nodded and said, "Only one from the great spirit can do that."

Starr seemed satisfied that this half of the problem was taken care of (at least for now), and so it was time to visit the ranchers and the cavalry.

She transported herself to the fort where the cavalry was assembling along with some of the ranchers. Marshall Fulton was there and was trying to talk some sense into the men that were there. As Starr appeared, a flash of light blinded the men.

The Marshall was very glad to see her and asked, "How did it go with the Indians? This is the first rain we've had in a long time. Did you have something to do with that?"

"As a matter of fact I did, sir," she replied. "That's what I used to convince them not to go on the war path. Since it had not rained in a while, all the animals and people on both sides have been competing for what water there was. The Indians are quite happy for the rain."

"Good thinking, Starr," he nodded.

He almost forgot to introduce Starr to everyone in attendance, though they decided to get out of the rain first.

"Starr, this is Captain Kline. He's in charge of this fort." Turning to Captain Kline, the Marshall said, "This is Starr Carpenter. She's a special agent with the US Secret Service and is on a special assignment from the President."

Starr looked at the Marshall with an odd look but began to understand his motives.

"The President knew of the trouble out here and asked Starr to see if she could mediate," continued the Marshall.

The ranchers and the cavalry officers were looking at Starr with a very strange look but listened to the Marshall carefully nevertheless. The Marshall was interrupted by a Sergeant who came in saying, "Excuse me for interrupting sir, but in all the excitement from the rain, Private Walker fell from the tower and broke his neck. He's dead, sir."

The Marshall looked at Starr and said, "Bring the Private over here right away. Starr is also a doctor and might be able to do something."

"Yes sir," replied the Sergeant.

In a couple of minutes, some soldiers brought the Private in the room.

Starr went over to him and placed her hands on his neck. She spoke to her computer and her hands began to glow. All the people in the room just stared and held their breath. In a few minutes, the Private jerked and began to breathe on his own. In another minute he opened his eyes, and Starr removed her hands.

"Now do you believe me?" asked the Marshall directing his question to the Captain and the ranchers.

They all nodded their heads.

"She can be just as deadly as she can be a healer," spoke the Marshall. "So keep that in mind."

Starr thought it was about time to speak up so she said, "It's my job to make sure that we have peace. What else do we have to do to have some for a while?"

One of the ranchers decided to be the spokesman for the rest and said, "I think you've already accomplished your mission since the rain should supply the water we need to keep all our herds happy for a while."

"Good," said Starr with a smile. "Let's try to keep peace as long as possible."

Starr looked at the Marshall and said, "I'll see you back in Tucson. I need to prepare for my journey back east." With that comment, she disappeared in a flash.

The Marshall spoke to the group he was with. "You haven't seen half of what she can do. She's quite a young lady, isn't she? "

The Captain nodded his head and said, "But can she cook?"

Starr was getting hungry and decided to get that pot pie and root beer, so she went to the saloon and talked with Katie.

"I hear you stopped the ranchers and the Indians from an all-out war," said Katie. "That's some mighty fine work for a teenager."

"Thank you, Miss Katie. This has been a good history lesson for me, though I should be ready to leave tomorrow morning as soon as the time warp circuits are repaired."

"I still think you're an odd young girl," Katie said shaking her head.

Starr smiled and said, "You're just not used to talking to someone from the future. By the way, this is great root beer. I should bring some back with me."

As soon as she said that, a rough looking man came in the saloon.

"Anyone know where the sheriff is?" he asked.

Katie stood up and asked, "Who needs to know?"

"Tell him Bart Sommers is looking for him."

Katie thought for a moment and said, "It was your brother, Joe, that held up the stage last week wasn't it? The Marshall shot him while he was trying to escape."

"Good memory lady," responded Bart. "I'm going to kill the Marshall like he killed my brother."

Katie looked at Starr hoping that she had some idea what to do.

Starr just sighed and followed the man outside as he walked back toward the sheriff's office.

The Marshall had just got back in town and was just about to get off his horse when Bart yelled out to him.

"Marshall, you killed my brother, and now I'm going to kill you."

Starr realized this had gone too far and decided to transform. She realized that it was not going to be a fair fight so as Bart drew his pistol, she energized a force field between the two men so that the shots from Bart were totally ineffective. Bart didn't know what to do and continued to fire, but it still had no effect.

The Marshall saw Starr and just smiled. "Bart, I'm placing you under arrest for attempted murder. Now drop your gun, and put up your hands."

Frank pulled out his gun and pointed it at Bart. Bart looked mighty surprised but complied by dropping his gun and putting his hands up.

Starr lowered the force field and transformed back to normal clothes.

The Marshall winked at Starr and brought Bart to the jail.

Starr decided to go back to the saloon and talk to Katie who saw the whole thing. Katie came up to Starr and gave her a big hug. "You're quite a girl," she said.

The rest of the day was uneventful, and Starr just did some reading till the next morning. She checked with the computer and realized there were only about 2 hours left before all the repairs were complete enough for her to travel home. She went downstairs into the saloon dining room and decided to have breakfast before leaving. Katie and the Marshall were talking about the events of the past couple of days. When Katie saw Starr she asked, "How 'bout some biscuits and gravy with some more of that sausage you liked?"

"Sounds yummy," said Starr with a smile.

Katie went off to get Starr her breakfast, and Starr looked at the Marshall. "Katie is a very nice lady. Have you given much thought to marrying her?"

This caught the Marshall off guard, and he seemed to even blush a little. "I've thought about it some. Do you really think it would work?"

"I've been noticing how she looks at you. I'll bet if you asked her, she'd say yes in a heartbeat."

The Marshall nodded and said, "Maybe I will at that."

A couple of hours later, the computer informed Starr that all the repairs were complete and that time travel was possible again.

Starr went to say her goodbyes to Jonathan, Katie, Doc, and the Marshall. The Marshall and Katie were holding hands, and Starr asked the Marshall, "Did you ask her?"

The Marshall said, "Yes, I did. Shouldn't it be obvious?"

Starr laughed and gave each of them a hug. "I know you'll make a great couple," she said.

Katie smiled and laughingly said, "We're going to name our first girl after you."

Starr just looked at them and said, "Oh, the poor girl."

That made them all laugh, and with that Starr transported back home for Christmas.

Chapter 9

Out of this World Trouble

"All Defiant astronauts, please report to the briefing room immediately," came the voice over the loud speaker.

The Defiant was a newly designed space ship that did not need rockets to get to an outer atmosphere. It carried enough fuel to get it into space with cargo, perform its mission and return to earth. What made this an exceptional ship was not only the technology but that it was designed, staffed, and manned with people from over two dozen countries. This was to be a mission of great importance for the world since it was truly a world event.

One staff member from each of the supporting nations came to the briefing along with their astronaut. The chief spokesman for the nations came up to the podium.

"This is a historic occasion," he said. "You astronauts are about to embark on a mission of cooperation for the welfare of mankind. We are all proud to be part of this venture. Each of you has a very important piece to play. Together, we will make history. Good luck everyone."

With that, the astronauts left the room and boarded the ship. There were 24 astronauts, and each of them had a piece of the mission to perform. They included the pilot, copilot, navigator, chief engineer, and 17 scientists of various types, a science teacher, a dietitian, and a doctor.

Once each of them was strapped in for take-off, the pilot went through the preflight checklist and the countdown began. Once the count was below twenty, the engines began to roar as the final checks were performed. The chief engineer counted the final ten.

"Ten, nine, eight, seven, six, five, four, three, two, one, zero, release all brakes."

The ship began to roll, and though the simulator had tried to be realistic, it couldn't match the acceleration of the real thing. At 140 knots the pilot pulled back slightly on the control stick, and the ship's nose-wheel left the ground followed by the main wheels a few seconds later. Once airborne, the wheels retracted and sealed themselves into the main body of the ship. The pilot then pulled back on the stick even further, and the ship began to accelerate even more as it climbed at about an 80 degree angle.

When traveling at better than Mach 10, it doesn't take much time to travel 100 miles, even if it is straight up. Thus within minutes they had achieved a high orbit around the planet, and within several more minutes they were outside earth's orbit altogether. Their mission was four-fold. The first was to be able to fly this new ship that didn't need rockets and could be reused. The second was to test the artificial gravity of the new aircraft. The third was to perform numerous scientific experiments. The fourth was to have this entire mission as a world venture of 24 countries. Thus far, everything was going according to plan.

"You all set for your fishing trip to the Yukon, Starr?" asked her father.

"I don't know dad," replied Starr. "I've been going over the packing list, and I still think I'm missing some things."

"You can always transport back here if you need something," said Matthew.

Starr sighed and said, "I'm trying to avoid that if at all possible. In fact, I'd like to think I could go without my communicator, but that's probably not wise. Jeff (Starr's boyfriend) and I should be fine. There'll be a guide, and he'll be in contact with his tour center at least daily."

Starr and Jeff caught a plane, and though there were several legs to the flight, they managed to get into the Yukon in only 13 hours. The guide met them at the airport, and it was another 6 hours before they managed to get to the outfitters outpost.

"This is pretty far out in the middle of nowhere," exclaimed Jeff to Starr.

Starr smiled, but the guide named Johnny said, "This is my kind of country. Nice and peaceful, where you can be one with nature."

"I can certainly understand what you mean, sir," said Starr nodding her head.

Once they left the outpost, the guide spoke up and said, "We've got about another 3 hours before we get to the fishing spot where we are headed. By that time it'll be getting toward evening, so we'll need to start making camp. We'll make it close to the lake, so we should be all set for an early morning fishing excursion."

Within a few hours they had made it to the lake. It was the most beautiful place that either Jeff or Starr had ever seen. There were mountains in the background, there were moose and elk on the opposite bank and large fish jumping out of the water.

All Starr could say was "Wow! This is like Christmas in July. It's beautiful."

"Attention, everyone. We've made it to our destination," spoke the navigator to the crew. "You can proceed with the experiments as planned."

The crew of the Defiant unstrapped themselves from their seats and began unpacking their science projects. Each of the crew had his or her own project, and only a few could be worked on at any one time. Most projects took several hours to perform, and others were to take several days. The ones that took the longest to perform were the ones that were set up first. Some projects could be performed in parallel while others needed to be performed serially.

The doctor of the group was in charge of any medications that might be necessary as well as any vitamins or other supplements. With so many countries represented, the dietitian had the job of making sure that each person received proper nourishment without being offensive to the country of origin. As it was time to eat, the dietitian began food preparations. What was special about this was that the cooking environment was not normal space food. The food actually was prepared on board the ship.

"This food is great," proclaimed the copilot. I've been on a lot of missions, but this food is easily the best I've had on any mission yet."

"I've got to agree," the scientist from Argentina declared. "Each of us has food that is acceptable that actually has flavor to it."

Everyone laughed and enjoyed their first meal in space.

The chief engineer spoke to the crew and said, "I'm going to run a check on the engines, so in case anyone's looking for me, I'll be in the engine control room."

The engineer walked back to the control room and closed and locked the door from the inside. He then began his work.

Though there were three separate systems for control of the engines, the engineer found all of them and sabotaged them to the point that repair was not possible regardless of what anyone did.

"There," he said. "So much for getting back and so much for peace. These countries will be pointing fingers at each other for a long time."

There were three tents set up for the night, one for Starr, one for Jeff, and one for the guide. Starr and Jeff were not yet married, so they made sure they each had their own space. Starr did some reading most of the night and just laid awake thinking about how it would be once she and Jeff were married. The night went without any problems and as morning broke, the sounds of the birds and other wildlife could be heard. Starr thought it was great.

Starr decided to get up when she heard Johnny start to rustle. She went outside, and the air was brisk, but it felt great to her. As the others came out of their tents they yawned and stretched.

"How's everyone doing this morning?" asked Johnny.

"I feel great," replied Starr.

"I think I have a little crick in my neck," replied Jeff "but I think I'm okay other than that."

Starr went over and gave him a little massage just in the right spot, and he said, "That feels great. Can you do that every day we're married?"

"I think I could do it if the price were right," laughed Starr.

Johnny fixed breakfast which consisted of some sausage and eggs that he brought with him along with some biscuits that he cooked over the camp fire in a little stove. When they were through, they packed up for a day of fishing.

"I'm going to leave my watch in the truck," Starr told Jeff. "I'd prefer not to be called while out fishing."

"Suit yourself," he replied. "We'll only be gone for a few hours before we'd likely be back for lunch."

After she took her watch off and put it in the truck, she got in the boat along with Jeff and Johnny.

"When will we be back?" Starr asked Johnny.

"Probably around five, for supper," he replied.

"What about lunch?" she asked.

"I have it in the sack," he replied.

Starr wondered whether there would be any world problems while she was out, but she hadn't heard anything at all while they were on the trip thus far. In fact, she hadn't had a call all week.

The doctor thought it was about time to have everyone take their supplements. He carefully opened the bottle containing the real supplements, ground them into a powder and threw them away. He then went to his belongings, opened a side pouch and pulled out another bottle that looked just like the original bottle and placed one pill with each glass of water that he poured. He smiled and said, "This poison will take a couple of days to work through their systems. It will not be detectable, and each person will just feel sleepy. They will not die for at least a week but they will be unconscious for several days. So much for a happy and prosperous venture among nations!"

When they got to their first fishing spot, Johnny unpacked their reels and laid out the bait. It was a good time of morning for fishing, and Starr decided to cast her line where she thought she had the best chance. No sooner had the bait hit the water, a fish grabbed it and she started fighting it.

"Whoa there," she said. "This has got to be a pretty big one. I'm pulling pretty hard."

Johnny looked over and smiled but then came over to lend a hand if needed.

"That seems like it'll be a good size fish."

After about 5 minutes of fighting, the fish started slowing down, and Starr started reeling it in a little more. Johnny looked surprised but put out the net to see what type and size this fish was. He yelled out and said, "This has got to be at least a 50 pound Muskie. Good job, Starr."

The navigator/communicator thought it time to begin his sabotage work as well. He snipped some of the wires on the comm link and the backup link. He also removed two of the chips from both the primary and secondary navigation units and destroyed them. "So much for peace," he said with a snicker.

⁂

"Hey, that's not fair," Jeff said to Starr. "You've caught five fish and I haven't caught any yet. How 'bout giving the rest of us a chance? It's almost noon and I'm starting to get hungry anyway. Maybe you could at least stop fishing while you eat."

Starr laughed and said, "Hey, I'm on a roll. Maybe you could take my pole while I eat. Who knows, maybe my pole is just lucky."

This made Johnny laugh pretty hard, though he wasn't laughing when Jeff caught his first fish with Starr's pole. Starr decided to be nice and let Jeff keep her pole and then decided to use his previous pole.

⁂

"Commander?" asked one of the communications officers at the Kennedy Space Flight Center.

"Yes," he replied.

"I've lost communication with the Defiant," said the officer.

"Continue trying, Lieutenant. Also, contact Houston, and see if they have any better luck."

"Will do, Commander," came the reply.

⁂

Aboard the Defiant, the crew members were getting quite sleepy and were almost unconscious except for the doctor. He wanted to wait till all were unconscious before taking his own life. Within another hour, the crew members were either asleep or in the doctor's case, dead. The ship was drifting out into space now well beyond the moon.

The fishing party had a wonderful day and was thinking about retiring for the evening as the sun was going to set in about another hour and a half. It would take at least an hour to get back to camp and by the time dinner was fixed, it would be time for bed.

"I still don't think it's fair that you got 12 fish, and I only got three," said Jeff.

Starr laughed and said, "We'll see who gets more tomorrow. Johnny, I've never tasted Muskie before. Any chance we can have some for supper?"

"I was counting on it there, little lady."

"Commander?" asked the communications officer at Kennedy.

"Yes," came the reply.

"Nobody has been able to reach the Defiant, and tracking has observed that the ship is drifting outside any flight path that was agreed upon."

"Get the President on the line," barked the commander.

When the President was on the line the commander reported the current status, "Sir, we have a situation here. There's been no response from the Defiant, and it's drifting off course."

The President thought for a minute and said, "Contact all the other staff members from the member countries, and see if they have any ideas. If not, we need to contact the countries themselves and inform them of the situation."

"Understood, Mr. President."

When the president got off the phone, he thought for a moment and then decided to contact Agent Thompson.

"Thompson, this is the President."

"Yes sir," came the reply.

"We have a situation here, and we may need help from Starr. Please contact her, and tell her that we've lost contact with the Defiant and it's started drifting."

"Right away, sir," came the reply.

The fishing party was about an hour from their camp when they saw two bull moose fighting on the shore.

"This is so cool," remarked Jeff. "How often do you see sights like that?"

"Every time I come out I see something different," replied Johnny. "Do you want to take any detours before we get to camp?"

"No, I think it's getting late enough, and I should check my communicator for any messages," replied Starr.

"Fair enough," said Johnny. "We'll be back in about an hour."

Agent Thompson tried calling Starr but didn't have much luck. He left a message and then decided to call her parents.

"Mr. Carpenter, this is Agent Thompson."

"Yes sir, what can I do for you?" asked Matthew.

"I'm looking for Starr. Do you know where she is?"

"She's on a fishing expedition in the Yukon out in the middle of nowhere."

"Can she still get reception where she is?"

"I expect so. She might not have taken her watch with her if she was going fishing somewhere special."

"Well, I hope we can get in touch with her soon. A lot of people may die in space if someone   doesn't get there soon."

Matthew thought for a second and said, "Let me see if I can activate the chip inside her arm. I might be able to make it vibrate and get her attention."

"Just do what you can to get her to respond ASAP," said the agent rather hopeful.

After they hung up from their call, Matthew went to the lab and powered up Anna (one of his medical healing machines) in an attempt to get the chip to vibrate.

The boat was still about one half hour out when Starr felt something funny in her arm. She looked at it, and the place where the chip had been inserted was moving. Starr thought for a second and realized that her father was attempting to communicate with her.

"Dad's trying to get hold of me," she said to Jeff and Johnny. "How soon can we get back to camp?"

Johnny thought for a second and said, "I can get you back in 15 minutes if I rev it up a little."

"Do it," replied Starr.

Fifteen minutes later, the party pulled into camp and Starr ran over to the truck to get her watch. She called her father who told her to contact Agent Thompson directly.

"This is Starr. What's the problem, sir?"

"The President has asked for your help. The Defiant is not responding and has started drifting. See what you can do."

"I'll get right on it, sir. Sorry about not being in communication range."

"Don't worry about that now, just get them some help."

"Yes sir."

Starr looked at Jeff and Johnny and said, "Excuse me for a while. I need to go find a spaceship."

With that she transformed and disappeared.

Johnny had never seen Starr transform before and didn't actually realize she was Starr Gazer. This caught him by surprise but Jeff calmed him down.

Starr appeared at the Kennedy Space Flight Center Defiant Mission Control Room. This startled everyone in the room.

"Calm down, everyone," Starr said. "I'm Starr Gazer. It would shorten the time for me to help the crew of the Defiant if you could get me a fix on the ship."

The communications officer spoke up first. "The last known coordinates of the ship are shown on the screen here, miss."

Starr went over to the console where the lieutenant was and scanned them in to her suit.

"Thanks, that'll help a lot," Starr said with a smile.

With that comment, she disappeared.

Starr reappeared in space and scanned for the ship. It had already drifted about 500 miles from the last know location the ground station had. She moved to just outside the ship and then transported inside it. She saw the crew on the floor and went to check them out. She got to the pilot first.

"Computer, analyze the patient."

"Patient has been poisoned with a slow acting drug."

"Can you repair him?"

"Affirmative."

"Go for it."

"Acknowledged."

Three minutes later, the pilot began to stir and awoke to Starr bending over him. He woke with a fright.

"Who are you?" asked the pilot.

"I'm Starr Gazer. You've been drugged, and the Defiant has been drifting. The President of the United States asked me to help you all out."

"Let me see what the status of the ship is. You go ahead and start getting the rest of the crew awake, and I'll be in touch."

"Who'd you like me to start with?"

"Start with this man. He's my co-pilot. I believe I can trust him."

Starr began reviving the co-pilot while the pilot looked over the ship. He determined that the navigation systems were out, the communications systems were out and the engines weren't responding.

Once the co-pilot was up, he began to work with the pilot to see what he could do to help the situation. Starr looked at the rest of the crew and determined that the only one that could not be revived was the doctor. From observation, it appeared like he had given himself a high powered drug that killed him almost immediately.

Starr went up to the pilot and said, "The others are still drugged, but the doctor appeared like he killed himself."

The pilot thought for a minute and nodded, "He couldn't have done all this by himself. He had to have help."

"Or there were others that were working totally independently," said the co-pilot.

"We can't risk the others waking up and undermining us again," said the pilot.

Starr responded by saying, "I can keep them unconscious but free from the drug. Will that work?"

"That would be perfect," replied the pilot with a grin.

Starr went to work on the crew while the pilot and co-pilot checked on how to get the ship operational. With a little repair work, the communication systems were repaired in a few hours. Starr looked at the navigation systems and realized that there were some pieces missing. With the communications working, the pilot radioed the command center on earth and advised them of the situation. Starr got on the radio with the pilot.

"I need a couple of chips from the nav systems to get them working again. Do you have anything I can get to quickly to get them operational? I'll transport back to get them."

The lieutenant at the command center responded saying, "We can pull what we need from the simulator."

"Good, I'll be there in a jiffy," replied Starr.

Starr transported back to earth and got the parts that were needed for the nav systems.

"Thanks, Lieutenant. I'll make sure the President knows how helpful you've been."

This made the officer smile and just say, "Thanks."

Starr transported back to the ship and replaced the missing parts.

"That takes care of the nav and comm systems. So what do we have left?" Starr asked the pilot and co-pilot.

We've got some problem with the engines. Neither of us in command has much experience in that area. We'll be glad to help, but we're not experts.

Starr went aft to where the engine control room was. She had her on-board computer run an analysis of the circuits and see where the problems were.

"Wires have been cut on the primary, secondary, and emergency backup starting circuits."

"It seems pretty delicate in those areas, how much can you do remotely?" Starr asked.

The computer didn't respond for about ten seconds but finally came back with, "If I reassign some of the medical repair circuits to effect the repair of the copper and insulation, it would be possible to repair these circuits remotely."

"How long will it take to reassign the internal circuits?"

"Four minutes twelve seconds."

"Do it, and then commence with the repair."

"Acknowledged."

Within ten minutes, the repairs had been completed on the engines, and the pilot decided to chance starting them. They fired up without any problem, and the pilot turned the ship for an earth approach.

Starr acted as navigator, as she could confirm an approach with her own on-board systems. The co-pilot acted as the communications engineer and performed the duties of the flight engineer. They couldn't risk bringing any other people to a conscious state since more sabotage couldn't be ruled out.

"I think we should get into an earth orbit before we attempt any sort of landing approach," said the pilot.

The co-pilot and Starr agreed to the pilot's thoughts and they continued along their flight path for another two hours before they entered an earth orbit.

The pilot and the command center agreed on an approach plan and the crew of three began their descent to earth. Under normal conditions they would have been able to land on any Air Force runway in the United States but they decided to land at Edwards AFB which would allow more flexibility in case of any additional problems.

"I think we're going to make it," replied Starr as they were on final approach at Edwards.

As they touched the ground, all three of the crew breathed a sigh of relief. Within ten minutes, there were ground crews available, and the doors were opened.

Starr asked the pilot to call for a security detail since an interrogation was in order. Once the security team was there, Starr began to revive the rest of the crew.

The pilot had a thought and said, "I don't expect that some of the people on the crew could have performed the type of sabotage that was done. I can probably eliminate some of them right away."

With that comment, he pointed to the ones that were not likely to have been the saboteurs. She revived those, and that left about five potential saboteurs.

Starr revived the other five and asked each of them some questions while monitoring their actions similar to a lie detector. She determined that the navigator and flight engineer were possible candidates. She turned them over to the security people with a note for further questioning with the likelihood of those being the saboteurs.

It was almost dawn by this time and Starr said, "I think you'll be okay. If you need anything else, give me a call."

The pilot smiled and said, "Thanks. We'd all be dead if it were not for you."

"I second that," remarked the co-pilot.

Starr sighed and said, "It's about time for breakfast. I'll see what's cooking on the lake."

With that, she disappeared.

Starr reappeared at the camp site and surprised both Johnny and Jeff.

"What took so long?" asked Jeff.

"That'll be a story for when we're bored out on the lake today," replied Starr. "Right now, I'm hungry."

Johnny replied saying, "One of the fish you caught yesterday is nicknamed *Defiant* in these parts since it's usually so difficult to catch. We cooked one up last night for supper and still had some left. Would you like some?"

Starr rolled her eyes and replied, "Suddenly I don't seem to have much of an appetite. Maybe I'll just go for an apple. Good thing this isn't really Christmas time otherwise I'd feel as if I was missing Christmas dinner."

Jeff and Johnny just looked at each other and shrugged.

Part III

The Second Xtreme Christmas

Chapter 10

Caught in the Past

Brad and Stephanie had been married almost a year. They were quite happy, and each of them grew in the Lord more and more every day. Brad continued to come up with ideas for new inventions, and the board of directors was very happy with making the billions of dollars that resulted.

One day while Brad and Stephanie were out on a date together (those sort of dates that couples have after they're married but before the children come along), Brad looked up in the sky and watched a fighter plane flying toward Andrews Air Force base. He nodded and said to Stephanie, "I'll bet I could design a fighter that could be better than anything there is now."

"I'm sure you could if you put your mind to it, honey."

"I think I'm going to come up with some ideas and maybe even run them by Starr and her father to see if I'm on the right track. I expect that they would be able to tell me in short order whether it'll work or not."

Stephanie pulled Brad close and gave him a kiss. "Does that mean there'll be a lot of late nights at the office for the next two years? We haven't even been married a year yet, and I'm probably already going to be a widow due to a workaholic husband."

He smiled and said, "I can do a lot of the design work at home. That should cut down on the missing husband syndrome."

Matthew and Starr were working on some more modifications to the suit when the phone rang. Matthew picked it up. "Hello, Carpenter residence."

"Matthew, this is Brad Crawford."

"Hello Brad. Haven't heard from you since you and Stephanie got married. How are you both doing? Any little ones on the way yet?"

"We're both fine and...no there aren't any little ones yet... that I know of."

"What can we do for you?" asked Matthew.

"I'm working on a design for a new fighter, and I'd like you and Starr to look over the plans. If I designed it right, it'll be the fastest plane in existence (better than Mach 10), and it'll turn on a dime. It'll also have some fancy new weapon systems that are way ahead of anything currently being used."

Matthew thought for a second and smiled saying, "We'd be honored to see what you're working on."

"Truthfully, Matthew, you and Starr are the only ones I'd trust to look this over. I think that anyone else would want to steal it."

Matthew was a little caught off guard with that remark but said, "I'm glad that you trust us enough to help. Just let us know what you'd like us to do."

"Can I come by tomorrow and bring everything with me?"

"Only if you bring Stephanie with you. I'm sure that Starr and Jennifer would love to see her."

"I'll do that," replied Brad.

"You can stay with us," added Matthew. "We have a spare bedroom for the two of you."

"That would be great. We'd appreciate the hospitality."

"Okay, we'll see you sometime tomorrow."

"Thank you, Matthew and goodbye."

After they both hung up, Matthew told Jennifer and Starr that they'd be having company tomorrow.

"Great," replied Starr. "I really like Stephanie."

"So do I," included Jennifer. "Now I've got to work on getting the spare bedroom straightened out, and I'll need to get the towels washed and a menu planned."

Matthew looked a little puzzled and said, "This isn't the President, Jen."

Jennifer just shook her head and said with a smile, "Men just don't understand these things."

Starr just stood there and laughed.

Brad got off the phone and told Stephanie what transpired. "What should I wear?" she asked.

Brad looked a little puzzled and said, "We're not going to the White House, dear."

Stephanie just shook her head and said with a smile, "Men just don't understand these things."

Brad was a private pilot with an instrument and jet rating. So when Brad and Stephanie woke up the next morning, they headed for the airport and took off in their private jet heading for North Carolina. Upon landing, they were met at the airport by Matthew who helped them with their bags and pointed them toward his car. The airport was rather noisy, so they tried not to say any more than absolutely necessary. Once they all were sitting in the car Matthew spoke up.

"How was your flight?"

"Pretty good," replied Brad. "The wind was to our back, so we made pretty good time."

"So tell me a little bit about these plans for the plane," said Matthew.

"Well, I've had this idea for a while – ever since Stephanie and I got married. Not that marrying Steph had anything to do with wanting to build a fighter," replied Brad.

Stephanie laughed and said, "He probably thought about it after our first fight. He probably wants to have the ultimate upper hand."

That just made everyone laugh.

The group continued with small talk until they got to Matthew's house. Once they arrived, Jennifer and Starr met them at the door. All the girls spoke simultaneously as they embraced each other.

"It's so great to see you," they all said at one time.

They all laughed as they came into the house.

"So what have the newlyweds been doing this year?" asked Starr.

"I'm not sure if that's an appropriate question to ask a newly married couple," interrupted Jennifer.

"It's okay," replied Stephanie. "We do what all people do. Eat, work, and sleep."

That made the entire group laugh.

Once the pleasantries were dispensed with, Jennifer and Stephanie went off to the kitchen to discuss dinner plans leaving Brad, Matthew and Starr alone in the living room.

Brad opened his laptop and brought up the set of plans for the new plane. He also had a hard copy available.

"If I'm right, this plane will be the fastest there has ever been with the most advanced weapon systems, sensors, and counter-measures," stated Brad. "It'll also have a very high powered combination sonic blaster/laser as a backup weapon that will have a two mile range."

Brad handed the plans over to Matthew and Starr for their perusal. Matthew held the book of plans while Starr watched. As he opened to the first schematic, he and Starr stared at it for about 15 seconds and Starr took her father's hand. There was a spark and then a whole series of sparks on their hands. This had not happened since Starr and Matthew had first designed her suit. This lasted for about 5 minutes during which Starr and Matthew closed their eyes. Brad was totally taken aback and didn't know what to do other than stare. Once the sparks went away, and Matthew and Starr opened their eyes, Matthew spoke up.

"Starr, you take the first half of the plans and I'll take the second half," said Matthew. "You know what to do."

Brad just looked dumbfounded but eventually asked, "Will someone please tell me what just happened and what is going on?"

Matthew decided to speak up first. "Starr and I will be marking up your plans based on the revelation we just got from God. This type of event hasn't happened since we first designed Starr's suit. I'm not sure why God chose to perform this miracle here, but the airplane design you have must have some far reaching significance."

Starr broke in, "I remember when this first happened. Dad and I were pretty shocked, in more ways than one. Dad's right, this would not have happened if there were not some big event or events that warrant the use of your invention."

Matthew started in again. "Starr and I will each take half of the plans and make appropriate changes to not only make sure everything functions properly but also add the changes that we were just told to make as enhancements."

By this time, Brad was totally blown away. He didn't know what to do or what to say so he just watched. It took about 2 hours for the plans to get modified as Brad watched Starr and Matthew work at lightning speed. While this was going on, dinner was getting prepared by Stephanie and Jennifer. Jennifer knew not to interrupt her husband and daughter while they were working but decided to at least tell them when dinner was ready. That happened to neatly coincide with the finishing of the plan modifications.

"Dinner's ready everyone," shouted Jennifer. She at least didn't have to worry about her other two children since Luke and Andrew were off visiting their grandmother for the week.

"What perfect timing you have," said Matthew as he got up and gave Jennifer a kiss. "We had another experience like the one we had when Starr and I first came up with the plans for Starr's suit. Remember when we told you about the shocking experience we had?"

Jennifer thought for a second and replied with, "Yes, and I remember the long days and nights you two had while you put the suit together. Does that mean I'm going to have to be another widow for a while?"

Matthew and Starr just laughed, but Brad and Stephanie just looked puzzled. As Matthew noticed the puzzled looks, he decided to speak up.

"When Starr and I get on a roll working, it's very hard to break us away. Jennifer tends to feel like she's been abandoned."

Now they all laughed. After this they all had a hearty dinner and sat down in the living room for some coffee and dessert.

"Based on your discussion before dinner, I expect you have some idea on how to proceed from here," said Brad.

"We don't want to take over your project," said Matthew, "but I think we should divide up the work. Starr and I can work on the software if you fabricate the hardware. We've modified the plans so you can easily see what's involved. We can get together via video conference on a daily basis if necessary. Do you have a private airport that can be used to house this beast when we get it all together?"

"As a matter of fact I don't but I'll work on it," replied Brad.

At that point they all retired for the evening. Brad and Stephanie went off to the Carpenters guest room and Jennifer went off to bed. Matthew went off to kiss Jennifer good night before staying up to work with Starr on the new project. By morning Matthew and Starr had a good start on the software and were ready to present Brad with their simulations of how they thought the fighter would work.

"You did all that in one night," exclaimed Brad. "It would have taken me months to even get some of it completed. You're good!"

Brad knew what he had to do and that he was going to be the furthest behind so he thought it best to get home and get started. Matthew took Brad and Stephanie back to the airport and then came back to continue work on the new project.

As the months progressed, both teams worked very hard to get their pieces of the plane built. They agreed to have all the on-board systems communicate with each other via a 10 gigabit fiber channel. This would be more than enough bandwidth to transport whatever data was necessary between systems. Everything was redundant including the force field that Matthew recommended. Though the airframe was made from a special titanium alloy which in itself would not stop an air-to-air missile from destroying the plane, a little extra insurance wasn't a bad idea. Another of Matthew's ideas was using a renewable energy source for the plane's main drive engine. This would eliminate having to refuel during an extended mission. For this, Matthew decided to use the same star power source as what Starr uses in her suit. This would also afford the plane a totally renewable source of power for some of the weapon systems. The plane also had the ability to perform vertical take-off and landing. This posed a different set of challenges but was worth the time considering it wasn't likely that an airstrip would always be available. Finally the day came for the first set of field trials.

"Since this is a two person fighter, who do you think should be the other person to be in on the field trials?" asked Brad.

Matthew knew right off that if there was going to be a problem that Starr should be the one to go since her suit would come in handy.

"I think Starr should go just in case any mishaps occur," indicated Matthew with a nod of his head.

"You're probably right," said Brad with a likewise nod of his head.

***

Later that morning Starr and Brad got into their flight suits and boarded the plane. When performing field trials on a new plane, the series of tests are rather elaborate. The tests in chronological order are as follows:

- Power up sequence
- Engine temperature and condition monitoring during high throttle sequences
- Exercising of the control surfaces
- Basic taxiing
- Rev up and acceleration up to the point of take-off but slow down prior to the actual take-off.
- Actual take-off but landing on the same runway without turns. This required a very long runway to allow for a high safety margin.
- Simple take-off with 4 wide turns completing a 360 degree turn and landing on the same runway
- Tests at various altitudes and power ranges
- Tests for the vertical take-off and landing system

- Tests for the various sensors and countermeasures
- Weapons tests
- Tests for the power refueling system
- Tests for the force field

The systems performed very well with only minor tweaking. Finally the day came for the super high performance tests. This was at a very high altitude and very high speed going around the world.

"Okay, Starr, you ready?" asked Brad.

"Yes sir. Ready as I'll ever be," replied Starr.

Starr and Brad were already in the plane and powering up when this conversation was taking place.

"Good," said Brad as he smiled and taxied out on the runway.

As Brad gave the plane half throttle he said "let's go for it."

The plane took off and Brad went at a very steep rate of climb and then pushed it to 75% throttle. The altimeter was increasing at close to 1000 feet per second and it was still handling like a dream. When they reached 100,000 feet they decided to level off.

"Starr, what do you think about pushing it to full throttle at this altitude?"

"Everything is within the safety margin, and we haven't seen any sign of weakening yet," she replied.

"Good. Here it goes," Brad said as he pushed the throttle to the maximum.

The plane hit Mach 10 and was still increasing speed when the automatic force field activated.

"What happened?" asked Brad.

"The force field activated because the software believes that the stress on the plane will be too much at this speed and altitude," she replied.

As she was about to elaborate, Brad noticed a strange phenomenon and told Starr to look at both her sensor instruments and just plain look outside. The instruments were indicating a strange electrical and magnetic storm that now seemed like it was all around them. As Brad was about to speak, the plane was hit by something unknown and the next thing Brad and Starr knew it was perfectly normal outside.

"What happened?" asked Brad.

"I'm not sure," replied Starr. "I was checking the instruments, but the readings were like nothing I've ever seen. I think we should communicate with dad and tell him we're coming back to the airport."

"I agree," replied Brad.

Starr attempted to open a communication channel but had no response.

"I'm not getting any response," said Starr. "I'm going to attempt to communicate with anyone I can via whatever channels are available."

"That's fine," said Brad. "In the meantime I'm going to slow down and get to a lower altitude probably something closer to 15000."

Starr began monitoring various communications and shook her head like something wasn't making any sense.

"Brad, I'm listening to some radio signals, and what I'm hearing doesn't make sense to me. What I'm hearing is also at very low power."

"I'm also seeing something pretty odd," replied Brad. "I've lost GPS and am working off inertials."

"Where are we?" asked Starr.

"Position Keeping indicates we're crossing into Germany," replied Brad.

"Brad," Starr said in surprise. "Look out the port window at 10 o'clock down a few thousand feet. Do you see what I see?"

"I'm not sure but I think those are B17s," Brad said. "What does the auto identification system indicate?"

Starr pressed a few icons on one of the glass touch screens.

"They're B17s all right. And the sensors are indicating other planes coming in. Getting a positive identification. Brad – these are German fighters. They're a combination of Focke-Wulf Fw 190s, Junkers Ju 87s, and Messerschmitt Bf 109s. Based on what we're seeing and the communications and the lack of GPS, do you know what I'm thinking?"

Brad knew what she was thinking and blurted out, "We're in the past somewhere in World War II, I think. What are the date and time indications on the stellar time indicator?"

Starr pressed a few more icons on a touch screens and said, "Looks like it's 0736 December 10th, 1944. That must have been some storm. I don't think I can transform in this time period since the suit is in a different time period."

Chapter 11

Guardian Angel

Brad just rolled his eyes and said, "Perfect. What do we do now?"

Starr looked back at the B17s and noticed that the German fighters were beginning to engage them. "Brad, I'm feeling as though we should be helping the B17s. I know this is a different time, but I swore to protect the United States interest no matter what. I just feel it in my gut."

Brad thought for a second and said, "That's good enough for me. Prepare all systems for battle. Arm weapon systems, and bring all sensors on line."

"Roger that."

Brad increased speed to Mach 2, enabled the force field and headed for the air battle already in progress. When Brad was within range of the first German fighter he fired and blew the antique plane to smithereens. There were about 25 fighters and he realized that the only way to get them out of the way quickly was to lock weapons on each of them and set the firing sequence to automatic. Starr saw what Brad was doing and nodded.

"You've got the right idea. That's what I do in the Starr Gazer suit when there are many targets."

Brad held his breath and pushed the button to fire. Immediately a series of flashes came from the airplane and within seconds all of the fighters were falling from the sky.

The pilots and crews of the B17s didn't know what to make of all this, and the mission leader (also called Red Leader) spoke on a secure channel to all the crews.

"Did any of you see what happened? I thought we were goners but it just seemed like all of the fighters blew up at the same time."

All the crews reported in, but none of them saw what happened.

"This is Red Leader. Though we don't know what happened, we need to continue on our mission and take out those enemy fuel reservoirs. Do you all understand?"

All responded in the affirmative.

"I feel as though we need to help them finish their mission," said Starr.

"Fair enough," replied Brad. "but we're going to need to stop and eat or do something like that after a while. I know the plane can stay up indefinitely, but we can't."

"Got that one loud and clear," said Starr. "Maybe we should contact the mission leader and tell him we're going to escort him till he's back home."

"Not too sure how well that would be received but we could give it a try," indicated Brad. "Here goes nothing."

Starr located the proper frequency and told the on-board computer to decipher the encryption algorithm thereby allowing them to break into the conversation. Starr and Brad listened to the chatter of the B17 crews and then broke in. Brad and Starr were far enough from the B17s that they could not be seen without the sensors that the aircraft of that era didn't have.

"Red Leader, hope you didn't mind some air support. We're on a special mission for the allied forces and noticed you were in trouble and without fighter escorts. We'll continue to escort till you're back in friendly territory."

"Who is this?" replied Red Leader. "This is a secure channel. We're on a top secret mission."

"We've blocked all exterior communications so your communications are quite secure at the moment. There isn't any other enemy aircraft within 100 miles, so you are free to continue on your mission. Based on your fuel supply and your current direction it appears that your intended target is a fuel depot 24 miles out. As I said earlier, we'll escort you till you're home."

"How do you know so much about our mission?" replied Red Leader. "What kind of technology are you using? I've never heard of anything that can do what you've indicated! We can't even see you!"

Brad and Starr smiled and decided to speak to each other on an internal channel before talking to Red Leader again.

"We should probably get close enough for them to see us so they're not totally paranoid," replied Starr. "Besides we're going to need some help eventually."

"Good thought," replied Brad.

Brad changed channel back to the B17 frequency.

"We'll get a little closer so you can get a visual, but we'll need to slow down quite a bit to stay with you," said Brad.

With that, Brad descended to the B17 level and came along side of the lead aircraft. The crews of the B17s all came to the sides where they could see the foreign aircraft. Brad and Starr waved to the crews and matched altitude and speed with the other aircraft.

Starr noticed the sensors flashing and decided to check the status. She noticed the antiaircraft guns directly along their flight path about 20 miles out. She decided to speak to Brad on the internal channel.

"There are antiaircraft batteries about 20 miles out along our flight path," said Starr. "We'll need to take them out. How about if you tell Red Leader what we're doing?"

"Roger that," replied Brad.

"Red Leader this is your Guardian Angel. Our sensors have picked up antiaircraft batteries about 20 miles out directly along our flight path. We've going to take them out. Guardian Angel out."

A confused Red Leader and crew just listened and watched as the advanced fighter increased speed to better than Mach 2 and then dropped altitude quicker than anything they had ever seen.

Brad maneuvered the fighter to an altitude of about 1000 feet and came upon the antiaircraft batteries totally by surprise. He fired on them with ultimate precision, and once the sensors indicated there were no other threats prior to the fuel targets, he guided the aircraft back to the flying bomber squadron. On the way, Starr spoke to Brad on the internal aircraft channel.

"I like that Guardian Angel title. We never did come up with a title for this aircraft. I think that would be as good a title as any."

Brad thought for a minute and then agreed with Starr.

"That's quite some aircraft you have, Guardian Angel," came a voice over the intercom. "I'm glad you're on our side."

Within a couple of minutes the B17s were over their targets and released their bombs. The explosions, fire and smoke were significant since the storage tanks were full.

"Would you look at that?" Brad said to Starr and the B17 crews. "Good job guys. Sensors indicate you've taken them all out. I'd say it's time to go home."

With that the planes turned around and headed for England. It took them about 2 hours flying time to get back, and when they were within 10 minutes of landing Brad and Starr thought it time to depart.

"Red Leader," spoke Brad over the radio. "this is your Guardian Angel. You're out of any imminent danger for the moment. We'll be in touch."

"Thank you for your help," replied Red Leader."

With that, Brad accelerated to Mach 3 and was out of sight almost immediately.

"We know their air field location, so now we just need to know what our next step will be," said Starr. "I think we need to contact Red Leader directly and talk to him so we can get some help deciding what to do next. I would normally talk to dad, but that's obviously out of the question at this point."

Brad thought for a second and agreed. "We are going to need some local help and the best way to do it may be someone that already knows something about us. I think I'll put us down close to the air field but out of sight. It'll be pretty easy to land using the vertical take-off and landing system (VTOL). I'm glad your dad suggested adding that to the *Guardian Angel*. Our advanced countermeasures will easily trick their primitive radar so we shouldn't have much problem with being detected. If we're quick enough, nobody should see us visually either."

"Hey! You're using our new aircraft name. Kind of catchy isn't it?"

"I think it's perfect," replied Brad.

With that, Brad landed in a small open area among a clump of trees, and once the systems were shut down they covered the *Guardian Angel* with a camouflage net for a quick disguise. They wrote a quick note on some paper that they had in their emergency packs, addressed it to the Red Leader who flew the B17 with the tail number that was on the lead aircraft and brought it to the main gate of the air field. They gave it to the guard on duty and asking that it be given immediately to the person to whom it was addressed. The guard looked at Brad and Starr with a very odd look but did comply with the request.

"I tell you General that was the most advanced aircraft I've ever seen," said Colonel Austin Gaar. "It wiped out the entire set of German fighters all at once and then took out all the antiaircraft batteries."

"If it's on our side, why haven't I ever heard of it?" replied General Richard Blake. "It's got to be some trick or some special weapon of the enemy. I've had calls in to Washington already, and they say they've never heard of anything like it, and all they're saying is that you're either drunk or fatigued."

"That would have meant that we'd have been all drunk at the same time," replied the Colonel.

There was a knock on the door.

"Come in," shouted the General.

A Corporal entered and saluted.

"Sir," said the Corporal. "A message for Colonel Gaar. This was received by the guard at the main gate."

The Corporal gave the message to Colonel Gaar, saluted and left the room.

The Colonel looked at the outside of the note and said to General Blake, "It's addressed to Red Leader with my tail number on it. The message says 'Glad you made it back safely. Please meet me outside the main gate at 6PM today - 1800 hours. Will answer your questions at that time. Please come alone. Signed – Your Guardian Angel.'"

The two men thought for a few seconds, and then the General spoke up.

"This has got to be a trick. I'll have a platoon of armed men ready to capture this man at 6PM."

"I think this is on the level sir. I'm willing to risk it," replied Colonel Gaar. "Remember that he could have taken us out just like he took out the Germans."

The General shook his head and disagreed but said, "I still disagree, but if you think this is on the level, you just make sure you call me every hour."

"I don't know if that'll be possible sir, but I'll call as soon as I can," indicated the Colonel. "I feel in my gut that this is the right thing to do."

"Just make sure your guts aren't spilled all over the country," smiled the General.

About 1745 Colonel Gaar requested a Jeep from the motor pool and had it brought around to his quarters. He drove outside the main gate, and as he exited the gate he saw a man standing on the side of the road about 50 yards away. He decided to drive over to him since the man seemed totally out of place.

Brad thought the man approaching in the Jeep seemed like the right one so he called out, "Red Leader?"

"People usually call me Colonel Gaar."

Brad extended his hand and the Colonel did the same. As they shook hands, Brad added, "People usually call me Brad, that's Brad Crawford."

"How do you do," came the response from the Colonel. "How about if you hop in and tell me what's on your mind?"

"That's fine," replied Brad. "At the same time we can go meet my copilot, and we'll tell you our problem. You can see the plane at the same time."

"Sounds like a plan. You just need to tell me where I'm going."

Brad directed him to where Starr and the plane were located and when they arrived, Starr met them at the Jeep.

Starr extended her hand and said, "I'm Starr Carpenter."

Brad added, "This is Colonel Austin Gaar AKA Red Leader."

Colonel Gaar noticed that Starr was a girl and that she couldn't be much more than a teenager.

"You can't be much more than 17," noted the Colonel.

"Very good," replied Starr.

"She happens to be one of the most brilliant people of the 21st century," said Brad.

The Colonel did a double take and looked at Brad and asked, "21st century?"

"That's right Colonel," replied Brad. "we're from the future. We were performing a high altitude test flight at 100,000 feet at better than Mach 13 when we hit some sort of electro-magnetic storm, and the next thing we knew we were thrown into your time period."

Starr then looked at the Colonel and added, "We really have a couple of problems, first we don't know how to get back to our time period, and second, we have no provisions to hold us till we can figure out a way to get back."

The Colonel thought for a minute and said, "I can help you with the provisions but I'm afraid I wouldn't know anything about your other problem."

Brad looked at the sky and said, "Before it gets dark we should go for a plane ride. What's the highest and fastest you've ever gone?"

The Colonel thought for a second and said, "I'd say about 20,000 feet at about 500 knots."

Brad smiled and said, "Hold onto your hat because we'll be well above those numbers. By the way, we'll be doing a vertical take-off."

Brad and Starr had the Colonel get into Starr's seat as she would be staying on the ground, and then she explained some of the controls and had him put on the helmet that allowed him to see some of the important instruments as well as the targeting information on the helmet transparent face. Brad started the engine and after the preflight began the vertical take-off. Having ascended to about 300 feet in the air, Brad spoke to the Colonel.

"I'm going to transition from vertical to horizontal flight and we'll be moving rather rapidly so don't be surprised."

"I understand," replied the Colonel.

With that Brad transitioned to horizontal flight by adjusting the airflow of the engines. He then turned off the auxiliary high powered fan used for balancing the plane eliminating any heat pockets that tended to cause some VTOL planes to be unstable. Brad accelerated to Mach 10 and climbed to 100,000 feet. He specifically did not go beyond Mach 10 this time.

"This is totally incredible," exclaimed the Colonel. "I can see the curvature of the earth at this altitude, and the speed is amazing. What's your power source?"

"We've captured the power of the stars. Actually this plane is not the first to do that. Starr is actually a real live super hero in our time and activates a suit that allows her to fly and have amazing weapon systems and sensors. The problem is that her suit is located in our time period and not in this one."

Brad thought for a few seconds and then added, "Let's slow down a little and get to about 40,000 feet and then I'll let you take over."

Brad brought Guardian Angel down to 40,000 feet, and slowed the plane some and then said, "Okay Colonel, see what you can do. Remember that this is a high powered plane and you're not likely to hurt it. A force field will come on automatically if you run into trouble and exceed the safety limits."

"I don't know what a force field is," replied the Colonel.

"It's a field of energy that surrounds the plane that stops it from being hurt – say from weapons of other planes," described Brad.

"Our B17s could use something like that," said the Colonel as he smiled.

The Colonel took the controls and began some simple maneuvers and graduated to some fancy ones like steep climbs, dives, and rolls.

"This is really amazing," said the Colonel.

"Can you think of some enemy targets that you'd like to take out?" asked Brad. "We could probably go do it now."

"There's a bridge we've been trying to destroy for a while, but we can never get close enough without lots of casualties."

"I'm game if you are," said Brad. "You lead, and when we're close enough I'll tell you how to arm the weapon systems and take the bridge out."

Colonel Gaar figured out his bearings and found his way to the bridge. They came in so fast that none of the enemy anti-aircraft guns and fighters could react at all.

"Okay Colonel. I'll enable the automatic targeting system that shows up on your visor. When the bridge shows up in the little square on your visor, push the red button on the control stick."

The Colonel followed directions to the letter and fired on the enemy bridge. It only took one shot and the entire bridge came down.

"Wow! Did you see that?" asked Colonel Gaar. "That was amazing and so easy. I need one of these for my squadron."

"Nice idea, Colonel, but this plane doesn't belong in this time period."

"I understand," replied the Colonel. "Thanks for giving me a taste of the future."

After a few more maneuvers, Brad took over and brought the plane back to where Starr had been waiting. She had been listening via her watch communicator which was tied in to the airplane communication system.

Upon landing, the Colonel said, "At first I wasn't sure whether to believe you, but after having flown the plane I realized that there is nothing like this technology in this time period. Now how about if we figure out some place for you to stay and get you something to eat. I know of a place to stay in town that also serves good food. I'll put you up there until we can figure out something else. I'll wangle some funds to pay for it."

"Until we figure out how to get home, we'll pay for our hospitality by working with you on some missions," said Brad.

"I could go for that," smiled Colonel Gaar.

The Colonel brought Brad and Starr to the hotel, got them each a room and made sure they had something to eat. The Colonel talked to the hotel manager and set up a tab for Brad and Starr to collect charges.

"I'll talk to you in the morning," said the Colonel. "It'll take me a little while to talk to the Commanding General tonight."

"By the way Colonel," said Brad. "Since we're on your side but don't want to give all the secrets away, we should keep any real dealings just between us."

"I think I understand the problem well enough to keep this as low key as possible. I'll let you know when the next mission will be."

After they all said goodbye, Brad went to his room and went to bed and Starr looked to see what was available to read.

"I tell you General, that was the most amazing experience I've ever had," said the Colonel. "I was flying at Mach 10 and at 100,000 feet."

The General looked at the Colonel sternly and said, "We need that plane. It would turn the tide of the war. You need to tell us where it is. We'll go over it with a fine tooth comb and I'm sure our scientists can figure out how it works."

"I don't think that's possible, General. The technology used to make that plane is far more advanced than anything our scientists are capable of in this time period."

"I disagree," replied the General. "I think we need to commandeer it."

"But they're willing to help us for as long as it takes them to figure out how to get back to their own time period. They're the designers of the plane and they are the only ones that really know how to handle it. They mentioned something about *software* and programming the on-board computer including the weapon systems, sensors, and countermeasures. I didn't even know what they were talking about until they showed me the plane's capabilities. There was something called a force field that allowed the plane to take a direct hit from as much fire power as the enemy could throw at it and have no damage."

The General thought for a minute and said, "They're willing to come with us on missions and help us?"

"Yes, General."

"Okay," nodded the General. "I may either get court martialed or get a medal for this. I'll take the gamble that it may be a medal."

"Great. When are we planning the next mission?"

"Day after tomorrow at 0500," replied the General.

"I'll let them know sometime tomorrow to be ready for 0500 the following morning," indicated the Colonel.

⁕

The next morning Brad and Starr went to the hotel restaurant to have breakfast. Colonel Gaar met them and they all had breakfast together.

"Where would you like us to meet you, Colonel?" asked Brad.

"We should take off around 0515 tomorrow so anywhere around that time should be fine. We'll be heading over the English Channel so we should be pretty easy to spot."

"We'll be there," indicated Brad.

⁕

"I see them on Radar," said Starr. "They're about 20 miles out heading 110 degrees. Looks like there's eight of them."

Brad opened a channel and said, "Red Leader, this is your Guardian Angel. Do you copy?"

"Red Leader here. I don't see you, Brad."

"We're about 18 miles to the south," replied Brad. "We'll meet you in a couple of minutes and stick with you the whole way. Sensors will let us know well ahead if we start getting any unwanted company."

Brad was traveling rather slow, something less than Mach 1, and he slowed down even more since he would need to match the B17s' speed until there was something for them to do. Once they met up with Red Leader and the rest of the planes on the mission, they crossed the English Channel and began entering enemy territory.

The colonel spoke on the intercom, "Our targets this morning are an oil refinery and a couple of bridges. We'll be making a wide swing around the north and then come in from the northeast. The refinery is first."

Starr noticed that there were planes coming in from the west and notified Brad that there were 18 fighters approaching. Brad opened a channel to the squadron. "There are some fighters on an intercept course to us. Starr and I will speed ahead and take them out. You can continue along your mission."

Brad increased speed to Mach 4 and armed all weapon systems. When the targets were within range to lock on the automatic firing sequence, Starr locked the weapons on the targets.

"Okay, Brad, you may fire at will."

Brad pressed the button on the control stick and a series of flashes came from the aircraft indicating that the weapons were in the process of firing.

The B17 squadron was approaching, and the crew members watched as the enemy aircraft blew up one by one in mid-air. Once all the enemy aircraft were destroyed, Starr watched the sensors for signs of anti-aircraft guns on the ground.

"Brad, I see something suspicious at 4 o'clock. Sensors have not yet identified what it is."

Suddenly Brad and Starr saw a flash and their plane was shaking violently.

"What was that?" asked Brad.

Starr ran some checks and came back with, "It was a guy with a bazooka on that low hill we just passed. Boy that was a lucky shot. Good thing the force field was on otherwise we'd be in several thousand pieces by now."

Brad came around 180 degrees and sent a missile at the hill where the bazooka was.

"So much for that trouble maker," said Brad.

Starr checked in with Red Leader and explained what happened. There were no other surprise events that day and the mission completed successfully.

Chapter 12

A Surprise Visitor

It was the week before Christmas 1944. Brad and Starr had been in the past about a week and a half. They had supported the B17 squadron most days and had wracked their brains trying to decide how to return home. Thursday December 21st 1944 Colonel Gaar met them at the hotel.

"I've heard there is a famous scientist in England," said the Colonel. "He's working on some special project for the United States."

"Who is he?" asked Starr.

"Some Jewish scientist called Einstein," replied the Colonel.

Both Brad and Starr immediately perked their ears up, and Brad decided to speak up.

"Dr. Albert Einstein is an expert in relativity and would be the perfect person to help us with our problem. We need to be able to see him."

Colonel Gaar looked a little puzzled and asked "What is relativity?"

Starr answered this one. "As speed increases toward the speed of light, time slows down, the mass of the object increases and the length of the object decreases. I can show you the equations if you're interested."

The Colonel shook his head, smiled and said, "No I'll just take your word for it."

Brad continued to push on meeting Einstein. "So what do we have to do to meet Dr. Einstein?"

"I'm not sure, but I'll check into it as soon as I get back to the base," replied the Colonel. "Is there anything else I can do for you?"

"The best thing we can hope for is to get a meeting with Einstein as soon as possible," said Brad. "Today would be best."

The Colonel got up, smiled and said, "Looks like I've got my work cut out for me. Besides, I know when I'm not wanted. So I'll just be on my way."

Starr just smiled and said, "Thanks, Colonel."

As the Colonel left the hotel and headed for the base, Starr looked at Brad and said, "This could be the right answer. We need someone to bounce ideas off of. I just hope he'll talk to us."

"The Colonel's pretty resourceful. I expect he'll pull through."

It took a few hours but Colonel Austin Garr proved how resourceful he really was.

"Yes. I'd like to speak to Dr. Albert Einstein," spoke Colonel Gaar over the base phone to one of Dr. Einstein's assistants. "Just tell him it has to do with some equations related to relativity and time distortion."

Colonel Garr was told to wait for a few minutes while the assistant relayed the message to Dr. Einstein. After what seemed like an eternity, Colonel Gaar heard someone pick up on the other end of the line and speak in a strange Jewish/German accent. "Hello, this is Albert Einstein."

"Hello, Doctor. This is Colonel Austin Gaar of the 63rd aero squadron."

"What can I do for you, Colonel?" replied Dr. Einstein.

Now the Colonel started to sweat since he wasn't sure what to say next. He hesitated for a moment and then took a deep breath and said, "I have a couple of friends that have been helping us with the war effort. They have a plane that travels better than Mach 10, and they are having some problems with the aircraft and asked for you by name for assistance."

"Why do they think that I would be able to help them?"

Now the Colonel started to sweat even more.

"Because they were caught in an electrical magnetic storm that caused them to be go back in time. In short doctor, they're caught in the past."

"This is all very interesting, Colonel but I really don't have time for jokes," laughed Dr. Einstein.

"This is no joke, Doctor," replied the Colonel.

"Goodbye, Colonel," spoke Dr. Einstein as he hung up.

"Rats!" exclaimed the Colonel.

"Okay time for a new approach," said Starr taking a deep breath. "I say we write out a few equations that Dr. Einstein and Dr. Wernher von Braun would have been working on about this time period, and then send Dr. Einstein a letter with that information in an attempt to show that we might actually know something and are on the level."

"I like it," said Brad.

"Okay here's some paper and a pencil. Let's get to work," continued Starr.

Starr thought for a second and said, "No I think we need to go a few years beyond where they are now. That way they might really think future and not present."

"I think you're right," replied Brad after thinking for a second.

Starr wrote the following on the pad of paper as she spoke the words. "We need equations or definitions for

- Escape velocity
- Eccentricity of an orbit
- Drag on a body
- Acoustic velocity
- Specific heat
- Thrust
- Momentum
- The angle θ from the periapsis point to the launch point required to pin down an orbiting object in space
- Second law of motion

Do you think that would be enough to pique his curiosity?" asked Starr.

"I think those should do the trick," replied Brad in an approving manner.

As the equations were being written out on the note paper, Colonel Gaar just shook his head and said, "This is all Greek to me."

Starr just laughed and said, "Only some of it is Greek such as π, φ, and θ. The rest is just basic mathematics."

"There's nothing basic about it," smiled the Colonel.

As Starr finished the last equation, the one for the second law of motion (F = dp/dt) she also wrote the plea to Dr. Einstein indicating their plight. As soon as she was finished she handed the paper to Brad who looked it over, and then Brad handed it to Colonel Gaar.

"Okay, I'll get this to Dr. Einstein with a way to contact me," said Colonel Gaar as he placed the paper in an envelope and headed out the door. "Goodbye all!" was the last thing he said.

The next morning as Brad and Starr were sitting in Brad's hotel room, there was a knock on the door. Brad got up to answer it and to his surprise, Colonel Gaar was at the door along with Dr. Albert Einstein.

"Well, this is a pleasure, Dr. Einstein," said Brad.

Colonel Gaar followed with the introductions. "Dr. Einstein this is Brad Crawford a scientist in the 21st century, and this young lady is Starr Carpenter also known as Starr Gazer who is claimed to be the most brilliant mind of the 21st century."

After everyone shook hands, Brad decided to get to the point.

"Doctor, Starr and I had been performing a test flight on an advanced fighter when traveling at better than Mach 13 we were caught in some electro-magnetic storm. The next thing we knew, we were here in 1944. Even though Starr is a modern super hero that can time warp with a special suit she wears, that suit isn't in 1944. The parts that would be required to build something like she wears have not been invented yet, so we're stuck here until we can figure out some other way to get back."

Dr. Einstein thought for a minute and said, "If there was some way to see exactly what happened at that time of the storm, there may be enough data to reconstruct the event."

Starr spoke up first and said, "Our black box recorder is pretty advanced and even takes visual recordings as well as thermal and other events that the sensors provide. Let's get to the plane, and we can show the good Doctor here what data is available."

With that, the group of four left the hotel and traveled to where the airplane had been hidden.

When Dr. Einstein saw the plane he just shook his head and said, "I only half believed you. I didn't know what would happen when we got here."

"How about if we start with a tour of the earth from about 100,000 feet," said Brad with a smile. "You up for a little ride, Doctor?"

Dr. Einstein smiled and said, "I think I would enjoy that very much."

Brad and Starr explained a little of the avionics and what Dr. Einstein could expect. They then helped him into one of the flight suits and helped him into the cockpit. Brad got in the other seat and began talking to the Doctor.

"The aircraft is powered by energy captured from the stars. We'll be ascending vertically till we're out of the trees and then we'll be accelerating to Mach 10 as we climb to 100,000 feet. Is there anything I can answer for you before we begin?"

"No. Right now I'm just taking it all in and enjoying every minute of it," replied the Doctor.

Brad performed the preflight and then climbed vertically for about 500 feet. He then transitioned to horizontal flight and began accelerating and climbing.

"Hold onto your hat, as the saying goes," said Brad. Within seconds they had passed 10,000 feet and Mach 2.

They increased speed to Mach 10 and then continued climbing until Brad leveled them out at flight level 1,000 (100,000 feet).

"So Doctor, what do you think of the earth at this height?"

"This is truly remarkable and a magnificent sight. The curvature of the earth can be seen, and it's very peaceful. Not like the surface where there is war, starvation and pain."

"I'm going to go down to around 50,000 feet and have you take over so you can feel what it's like to fly something of this type," said Brad.

Brad started to descend and when he reached flight level 500 (50,000 feet) he told his passenger to take over the control stick. As Dr. Einstein took over, Brad made sure he kept his hands and feet close to the controls just in case he needed to recover from any problems quickly.

"I'm not sure I can do this, Brad."

"Just take it easy, and don't make any sudden moves," replied Brad. "Don't worry. I'll take over if I find you are going to crash." The both of them laughed at that remark.

The Doctor took Brad's advice and moved the controls slowly at first and eventually began to feel more at ease. He climbed, rolled and banked with more and more confidence.

"I feel like a child with a new toy," Dr. Einstein said with something of a giggle in his voice.

"I'm glad you're having a good time," replied Brad.

After a few more minutes, the Doctor smiled and said, "So that you don't think I've been ignoring your problem while I've been up here enjoying myself, I have some ideas that I'd like to talk about when we get back on the ground."

"I'm sure we'll all be interested in what your thoughts are," said Brad.

After another half an hour, Brad and his "pilot trainee" returned to where Starr and the Colonel were waiting.

Starr rigged up a way to look at the recorded data from the black box flight recorder. She went back to the exact date and time where the time change took place. This was the point where they were about to increase their speed beyond Mach 10. All four of the people (Starr, Brad, Colonel Gaar and Dr. Einstein) watched the data as it was brought up on the computer screen. Dr. Einstein was particularly interested in the effects of the storm as the plane went through it and then the other three saw him smile.

"I have a theory based on what I am seeing on this device you call a computer," said the Doctor. These numbers here are the results of Maxwell's equations are they not?"

"That's correct, Doctor," replied Starr.

"I believe that storm is not really a storm at all like you would normally think of a thunder storm but a stationary electro-magnetic effect that will affect whatever passes through that space at some high speed," remarked the Doctor. "If you would have gone through at a slightly different speed or altitude or the time you remained at that speed and altitude were different, the place in time you would have ended up could have been quite different. Thus I believe there to be a range of speeds and altitudes that could work to get you home, but without years of analysis and testing I believe the best answer to your problem will be to do a complete reversal in time and space of the exact journey you took to get here. This recording device of yours, which is truly quite remarkable in its own right, has all of the vital parameters recorded for exactly when you changed speed, altitude, latitude and longitude as well as many other parameters that could be important. I recommend you find a way to totally reverse the course that brought you here and see if that works. I feel that this approach would have a high probability of success."

Starr and Brad looked at the data that Dr. Einstein had been looking at, and then they looked at each other and shook their heads in the affirmative.

"I believe you're on to something, Doctor," replied Starr. "I should be able to program the on-board navigation/auto-pilot computer to retrace our steps with a very high level of detail. With a little luck and a lot of prayer, I think we could be home soon."

"With that said, I think I should be getting back to London and my current project," said Dr. Einstein.

"Thank you very much for your help, Doctor," said Brad as he shook Dr. Einstein's hand.

"That goes for me too," said Starr. "On a side note - from what we know of history, the Manhattan Project will turn out fine."

Dr. Einstein looked quite surprised that Starr knew of the secret project.

Starr then pulled out something as a present for Dr. Einstein.

"While you were having fun in the sky I found a way to get you something special for helping us out."

It was a tee shirt with the following equation written on it in very large print: $E=mc^2$. The following saying was written below it: ***I wrote this equation for energy and I'm just full of it.*** Below that was Albert Einstein's signature.

Dr. Einstein just smiled and then started laughing. "I love it!" was all he could say.

With that, the group said their final goodbyes, and then Colonel Gaar took Dr. Einstein back to London.

It was Christmas Day 1944, and Starr had completed all the preparations for the trip. The auto pilot and navigation system had been programmed with all the data from the flight data recorder that was necessary to perfectly reverse the course that got her and Brad to that time period. Colonel Gaar had arrived early in the morning (about dawn) in order to say goodbye.

"It's been a pleasure knowing you, Colonel," said Brad as he shook the Colonel's hand.

"Likewise," replied the Colonel.

"As soon as we get back to our own time period and get settled, I'll come back for a visit," said Starr. "I'll probably come by today sometime."

"Today?" asked a confused Colonel.

"This is time travel Colonel, I can come back to whatever time I like," Starr said with a smile.

Colonel Gaar initially looked puzzled, but after thinking about it for a minute nodded his head and said, "Okay, I think

I understand. Time in your time period has no relationship to time here."

"Very good, Colonel," replied Brad. "We'll make a scientist out of you yet."

The Colonel shook his head and with a smile said, "I'm a pilot. I never have learned to do two things at the same time."

At that point Brad and Starr put on their flight suits and entered their *Guardian Angel* while waving their final goodbye.

The *Guardian Angel* was about at Mach 10 and closing in on 90,000 feet following the pattern that Starr had programmed into the navigation and autopilot systems.

"We're about to cross over the point where we had decreased speed after the storm," said Starr. "We should prepare ourselves as the autopilot increases our speed to Mach 13+. As soon as that happens we should be in the electro-magnetic field and should wait till the autopilot drops our speed back to Mach 10. At that point we should be back in our own time period."

"I understand," said Brad. "I think I'll just pray."

In less than a minute the autopilot changed speed to better than Mach 13 which was the speed that Brad had previously taken the plane. As expected, the electro-magnetic force showed up, and within another minute the speed of the plane slowed to Mach 10.

"Our GPS is back," exclaimed Brad.

"And our automatic time keeper indicates the same time that we left our time period," replied Starr in an almost ecstatic tone. "Thank you, Lord, and thank you, Dr. Einstein."

"Okay, now let me get us back to the airfield," said Brad. "I can't wait to see Stephanie."

Upon arriving home Starr breathed a sigh of relief and decided to sit down and talk to her parents.

"So, how was the flight?" asked her mother. "Anything interesting happen?"

"Well, we went through an electro-magnetic effect which we thought was a storm and ended up in 1944. We used the aircraft to help out the Allied forces and met a lot of cool B17 squadron personnel. We couldn't figure out how to get back to our time so we happened to meet up with Dr. Albert Einstein who looked at our black box flight recorder data and gave us a recommendation on how to get back here. He was right on the money, and we got back in one piece. Would you like any more details?"

Matthew and Jennifer just stared at Starr with their mouths open.

Upon arriving at his house Brad breathed a sigh of relief and decided to sit down and talk to Stephanie.

"So, how was the flight?" asked Stephanie. "Anything interesting happen?"

"Well, we went through an electro-magnetic effect which we thought was a storm and ended up in 1944. We used the aircraft to help out the Allied forces and met a lot of cool B17 squadron personnel. We couldn't figure out how to get back to our time so we happened to meet up with Dr. Albert Einstein who looked at our black box flight recorder data and gave us a recommendation on how to get back here. He was right on the money, and we got back in one piece. Would you like any more details?"

Stephanie just stared at Brad with her mouth open.

There was a very bright flash in the mess hall where Colonel Gaar was finishing Christmas dinner. Starr was there in her street clothes as she had performed a double transformation (time transfer and then an almost simultaneous deactivation of her Starr Gazer suit). The suit stayed in the correct time period with her this time.

"Hello, Colonel. Dr. Einstein's theory worked. We did manage to get back to our own time period."

"Well that's wonderful," replied the Colonel.

"I've got a couple of presents for you, Colonel," said Starr.

Starr opened a bag that she had and pulled out several wrapped Christmas packages and gave them to Colonel Gaar.

"Wow, this is a surprise," he said. "Let's see what you brought."

He opened the first package which was a book written in 2010 on the aircraft of World War II. It was very large and in color with great descriptions of the aircraft.

"This is incredible," he said as he opened it up and scanned through the pages. "I'll be spending some time looking at this."

Colonel Gaar showed it to some of his companions who happened to know of Starr and Brad as they were on some of the missions.

The Colonel opened the second package and saw that it was a colorful printed tee shirt with a B17 in combat mode dropping bombs.

"This is very nice. I like it," said the Colonel in an approving manner.

He opened the third present and didn't know what to make of it.

"This is a family tree," said Starr. "I knew that the Carpenters and the Gaars were related, so I traced out how you are related to me. You're actually one of my distant cousins."

"Well I'll be," was all that the Colonel could say. After a few seconds he added, "I'm actually related to a real live super hero."

After the laughter died down, and the group said their goodbyes, Starr transformed into her Starr Gazer suit and disappeared.